THE PILGRIM'S PROGRESS

A JOURNEY RETOLD FOR TEENS

(BOOK ONE)

JOHN BUNYAN

edited and retold for teens by
CYRIL OPOKU

Published by **Quest Publications**

First Printing: 2025
ISBN: 978-1-988439-50-1

Cover design and interior layout by **Quest Publications**
Printed in United States of America

For more resources or to contact the author, email: questpublications@outlook.com

Disclaimer: This book is a creative and modern retelling of *The Pilgrim's Progress* by John Bunyan, adapted for contemporary teen readers. While care has been taken to maintain theological integrity, it is not intended to replace Scripture or formal doctrinal instruction. Any views expressed in commentary or interpretation are those of the editor and do not necessarily represent the original intent of John Bunyan or the publishers of the cited Bible versions.

Contents

Editor's Preface

When John Bunyan penned *The Pilgrim's Progress* over 300 years ago from a prison cell, he never could have imagined the impact his story would have on generations of believers across the globe. Told through vivid allegory, Christian's journey from the City of Destruction to the Celestial City has inspired countless readers to examine their own spiritual walk with God. But for many teens today, the language and style of the original work can feel like a barrier—something distant, outdated, and difficult to relate to.

That's where this edition comes in.

This *Teen Edition* of *The Pilgrim's Progress* was created with a clear purpose: to bridge the gap between Bunyan's timeless message and today's youth. Every chapter has been rewritten in modern language without sacrificing the power, depth, or beauty of the original. We've paired the story with thoughtful commentary from a teen's point of view—sometimes raw, sometimes humorous, but always real. Along the way, readers are invited to stop, reflect, and connect what they're reading to Scripture and their own faith journey.

My hope is that this edition makes *The Pilgrim's Progress* feel alive and urgent again—because the truths it contains are just as relevant now as they were centuries ago. In fact, perhaps more so. Teens today are navigating a world filled with distractions, pressures, doubts, and conflicting messages about truth, identity, and purpose. In the middle of all that, Bunyan's story offers a compelling reminder: you're not alone, your struggles have meaning, and there is a path that leads to life.

Whether you're reading this book for the first time or rediscovering it in a new light, we pray it inspires you to walk more boldly, love more deeply, and follow Jesus more faithfully—no matter what obstacles you face.

Let the journey begin.

— *Cyril Opoku*
(May 2025)

BUNYAN'S BEHIND-THE-SCENES CONFESSION

It started as a side project. A brain break. Nothing fancy—just late-night scribbles on the back of an old notebook when the world got too loud and his thoughts too heavy.

John wasn't trying to write a bestselling book. He wasn't chasing followers or likes or the approval of literary critics. Honestly, he was just trying to make sense of what it meant to follow Jesus in a world that didn't make it easy. Writing helped him quiet the noise.

"I didn't mean for this to turn into *something*," he later explained. "I was working on a totally different project. But then this idea grabbed me—this picture of the Christian life as a journey. One image led to another, like sparks flying from a fire."

Soon he had characters. Places. A plot. A pilgrim carrying a burden. A distant land. A gate. A cross. And choices—so many choices.

The story built itself like a house he didn't know he was constructing. He looked down at the pages, surprised at how full they'd become. But then came the harder part—should he *share* it?

People he trusted gave mixed reactions.

"This is genius!"

"This is too weird."

"Print it!"

"Please don't."

John found himself stuck in that awkward space between confidence and self-doubt.

"What if no one gets it? What if they laugh? What if it's too dark? Too symbolic? Too... different?"

But then another thought crept in:

"What if someone actually needs this? What if God's truth can shine through my weird metaphors and strange dreams?"

So he took a risk. Not because he was sure everyone would love it—but because he *hoped* someone might see themselves in it. Someone might feel less alone. Someone might finally understand the weight they're carrying—and where to lay it down.

—John Bunyan

Teen Commentary

Bunyan's intro is basically the original *"So this might be dumb, but…"* followed by him dropping one of the most powerful Christian books *ever.*

He didn't think it was impressive. He wasn't trying to impress. He was just trying to be *real.*

That's huge. Because maybe you've felt like your story doesn't matter. Or that your creative ideas are too "out there." Maybe you're scared to speak up about your faith because you're afraid of what people will say. Bunyan *gets* that.

But here's the truth: God can use your weird, imperfect, honest story. In fact, sometimes the most powerful messages come wrapped in unexpected packaging—dreams, poems, metaphors, or TikToks that hit you right in the soul.

You don't have to be a pastor or a theologian to share your journey. Just be brave. Be real. Share what God's doing in your life, even if it feels small or unfinished. You never know who might need to hear it.

Reflection Questions

1. Have you ever felt like your story or your faith isn't "good enough" to share? Why?

2. What's one creative way you could express your journey with Jesus—writing, music, art, conversation?

3. What holds you back from being real about your faith with others?

4. Who's someone in your life who might need to hear a story like *yours*?

Scripture Connection

"We now have this light shining in our hearts, but we ourselves are like fragile clay jars containing this great treasure. This makes it clear that our great power is from God, not from ourselves."—*2 Corinthians 4:7 (NLT)*

Devotional Prayer

Jesus, thank You for using ordinary people to tell extraordinary stories. Help me not to hide my journey just because it feels messy or unfinished. Give me courage to speak, write, and live in a way that points to You—even if it's not perfect. Use my story to encourage someone else, and let Your truth shine through it all. Amen.

Introduction

THE DREAM THAT CHANGED EVERYTHING

I t all started with a dream.

Not the kind you forget the second you wake up. This one felt real—like stepping into another world where everything mattered more than it does here.

In the dream, I saw a man.

He wasn't some brave hero or famous influencer. He looked ordinary—jeans, hoodie, sneakers. But his face? You could tell something was eating him up inside. His eyes were tired, his shoulders hunched, and on his back... was a backpack so big and heavy, it looked like it should've crushed him.

He was holding a book in one hand and mumbling to himself like he was desperate to understand it.

"What's wrong?" I asked, though I don't think he heard me.

The man suddenly dropped to his knees, groaning. "What should I do?" he cried out, voice shaking. "Is there any way out of this?"

He stumbled home, but even there—surrounded by his family—he couldn't sit still. He paced the floor, stared out the window, held the book to his chest like it was the only thing keeping him together. He tried explaining the burden, but his wife and kids just gave him that *you're acting weird* look. They told him to calm down, get some rest, maybe take a break from reading so much.

But he couldn't.

That night, he stood outside, eyes locked on the sky, like he was waiting for an answer to fall from heaven.

And that's when the journey began.

Teen Commentary

Okay, so it starts with a *dream*—but not like flying or failing your math final. This dream is more like those moments in real life when something finally *clicks*. You realize things aren't okay, and you can't fake it anymore.

The man in the dream? He's like a lot of us. He knows something's wrong inside, even if everything on the outside looks normal. He feels *heavy* with guilt, questions, confusion—and he can't ignore it anymore.

This whole book kicks off because one guy decides he won't pretend anymore. That takes guts. He's willing to look foolish, even to the people closest to him, because he wants truth and freedom more than comfort and fake peace.

That's where real journeys begin.

Reflection Questions

1. Have you ever felt like something was "off" inside, even if no one else could see it?

2. What do you usually do when you feel overwhelmed or spiritually lost—do you numb out, distract yourself, or ask for help?

3. How do you think people might react if you told them you were trying to take your faith seriously?

4. What's one small step you could take today to move closer to God—even if others don't understand?

Scripture Connection

"My guilt overwhelms me—it is a burden too heavy to bear."— *Psalm 38:4 (NLT)*

Devotional Prayer

God, sometimes I feel heavy—like there's a weight on my heart no one else sees. Like the man in the dream, I carry burdens I don't know how to unload. Thank You that You understand even the parts I struggle to put into words. Help me to be brave enough to stop pretending everything is okay, and to bring my confusion and guilt to You. Give me courage to take small steps closer to You, even if it feels awkward or scary. Remind me that You are near when I'm overwhelmed, and Your grace is enough to carry my load. In Jesus' name, Amen.

Scene 1

EVANGELIST PROVIDES DIRECTION

Christian stood alone in the dim evening light, staring at the sky like it might have answers. The weight on his back—this invisible, crushing burden—seemed to grow heavier with every heartbeat. His house was behind him, warm lights in the windows, the muffled laughter of his family inside. But he couldn't go back. Not like this. Not with this feeling in his soul that something was terribly wrong.

He buried his face in his hands, shoulders shaking. "What am I supposed to do?"

"Looking for something, are we?"

Christian jerked his head up. A man in a long coat stood on the edge of the road, leaning slightly on a walking stick. His eyes were kind but piercing, like he saw right through Christian.

"I... I don't know," Christian admitted. "Something's wrong with me. I feel like I'm carrying... guilt. Fear. Like this giant weight I can't shake off. And I keep reading this book—" he held up a battered Bible, "—and it says judgment is coming. I want to escape it, but I don't know how."

The stranger nodded slowly. "Name's Evangelist. And you're not crazy. That burden? It's real. And you're right—it won't go away on its own."

Christian swallowed hard. "So, what do I do?"

Evangelist pointed toward a distant hill, its peak barely visible through the evening haze. "You see that light over there?"

Christian squinted. "Maybe…"

"Follow it. Straight ahead. Don't stop, no matter who tries to distract you. That road leads to the narrow gate. There you'll find the beginning of everything you're looking for—freedom, forgiveness, purpose."

Christian hesitated. "What if I get lost?"

"You'll be tempted to turn around. Some people will say you're being foolish. Others might try to pull you in different directions. But keep your eyes on that light. And remember, you're not alone."

Christian took a deep breath. He looked one last time at his house—his past. Then he turned toward the light.

And took his first step.

Teen Commentary

Ever feel like something's off, but you can't explain it? That's what Christian was going through. He felt the weight of guilt and the fear of judgment, but didn't know what to do about it—until someone pointed the way.

Evangelist is that wise voice we all need sometimes. A mentor. A youth leader. A parent. Or even just that quiet nudge in our heart saying, "Hey, this isn't all there is."

The light Christian sees? That's hope. Direction. Truth. Sometimes following it means leaving comfort behind. But if we keep our eyes on it—on Jesus—we'll find something better than comfort: **freedom**.

Reflection Questions

1. Have you ever felt like Christian—burdened, but unsure why?

2. Who are the "Evangelists" in your life—people who point you toward what's right?

3. What's something you may need to walk away from to follow God more fully?

4. What's one "light" you can focus on when life feels dark or confusing?

Scripture Connection

"Enter through the narrow gate. For wide is the gate and broad is the road that leads to destruction, and many enter through it. But small is the gate and narrow the road that leads to life, and only a few find it." —*Matthew 7:13-14 (NIV)*

Devotional Prayer

God, sometimes life feels confusing and I don't know which way to go. Like the pilgrim meeting the Evangelist, I need someone to show me the right path when I'm lost. Please guide me with Your truth and help me listen when You speak. Give me the courage to follow Your direction— even when it's hard or different from what others want. Help me trust that Your way leads to real life and peace. Thank You for never giving up on me. In Jesus' name, Amen.

Scene 2

OBSTINATE AND PLIABLE

Christian's sneakers slapped against the pavement as he ran down the street, backpack bouncing, breath tight in his chest. His eyes were locked forward, focused on something no one else could see—something that had gripped his heart and wouldn't let go.

Behind him, voices rose. Shouts. Laughter. Mocking.

"There goes Chris! What's he doing—running away from life?"

"Where you headed, Bible Boy? Youth group retreat?"

More laughter. Someone whistled sharply, trying to get him to turn around. A few neighbors stormed out of their houses, waving their arms. Two of them, Obstinate and Pliable, started jogging after him.

Christian heard them before he saw them. "Chris!" Obstinate barked. "Get back here, man! What are you even doing?"

He slowed slightly, enough to let them catch up, but not enough to stop moving forward.

"Guys, I can't go back. I *won't*. I've seen the truth—I know what's waiting for me if I stay in that place."

Pliable looked confused. "What are you talking about? You're leaving everything—your friends, your family, your comfort—for... what exactly?"

"The city we live in—it's broken," Christian said, slowing to a walk but still heading down the road. "It might look fine now, but it's heading toward destruction. I've read it. I *feel* it. I'm on my way to a better place—something eternal. Something real."

Obstinate rolled his eyes. "So you're abandoning everything for some fantasy? You're seriously ditching the life we've got for something you *hope* is better?"

Christian turned, eyes fierce. "It's not a fantasy. I've read the Book. I believe the promise. What I'm chasing is worth more than anything I'm leaving behind. You can come with me. There's more than enough for all of us."

Pliable glanced between the two. "Wait… you really think there's something better out there?"

Christian nodded. "An inheritance that never fades. It's being kept safe—*for us*. I'm not guessing. I'm trusting the One who promised it."

Obstinate crossed his arms. "So, what—you're some kind of preacher now? Save the sermon. I'm not giving up my life for some vague hope. I'll stick with what I know."

"Come on, Pliable," Obstinate added. "Don't waste your time. Let's go back."

But Pliable hesitated.

"I don't know… What Christian is saying—it actually makes sense. If what he says is true, it *is* worth it."

Obstinate groaned. "Seriously? Don't be gullible. He's brainwashed."

Christian held out his book. "Read it for yourself. The promises in here are sealed with the blood of the One who made them. He gave everything so we could have this hope. I'm not crazy—I'm committed."

Obstinate scoffed and turned around. "You two are fools. I'm done with this."

Christian and Pliable kept walking, side by side now.

"So… you know where we're going?" Pliable asked.

"Not exactly," Christian admitted. "But a man named Evangelist gave me directions. There's a narrow gate just ahead. That's where we'll start."

Pliable nodded slowly. "Then let's go."

And together, they walked toward a new beginning.

Teen Commentary

This moment in *The Pilgrim's Progress* is *peak drama*. Imagine running full speed toward something you *know* matters—your heart pounding with excitement and fear—only to have your old friends chase you down, yelling at you to come back.

That's Christian's moment. He's made up his mind to follow God, and the people closest to him just don't get it. One mocks him (Obstinate), and the other (Pliable) is on the fence. This is the tension many teens feel when they decide to live for Jesus: people around them won't always support the choice.

But here's the key: **Christian doesn't back down.** He stays kind, but firm. He knows what he's after—something eternal, real, and worth everything.

Sometimes following Jesus means walking away from what's familiar, even from people who don't understand your faith. It's not about being better than anyone—it's about knowing there's more, and choosing to chase it.

Pliable? He's curious but not convinced. (Spoiler alert: he doesn't stick around for long.) Obstinate? He's loud, proud, and stuck in his ways.

So here's the big question: **who are you walking with?**

Reflection Questions

1. Have you ever felt like people didn't understand your faith or made fun of your beliefs? How did you respond?

2. Which friend are you more like right now—Christian, Pliable, or Obstinate? Why?

3. What's one comfort or habit you might need to leave behind to chase after Jesus more fully?

4. Who are some people in your life who help you keep walking toward God?

Scripture Connection

"We fix our eyes not on what is seen, but on what is unseen, since what is seen is temporary, but what is unseen is eternal."
—*2 Corinthians 4:18 (NIV)*

Devotional Prayer

Jesus, I want to follow You—even when it's hard, even when others don't understand. Give me courage like Christian, and help me walk with people who push me closer to You. Help me let go of the things that hold me back, and trust You for what's ahead. Amen.

Scene 3

THE SLOUGH OF DESPOND

The trail started off okay—muddy, but manageable.

Christian trudged forward, his massive backpack bouncing with every step. His friend, Pliable, had decided to come with him. After hearing about the Celestial City—this perfect place free from pain, full of joy and life—Pliable was all in. No hesitation.

They were laughing a little, trading guesses about what this City would be like, when it happened.

One step. Then another.

Then—**SPLASH.**

The ground turned into a swamp.

Thick, dark muck sucked at their legs like quicksand. Christian slipped and fell, face-first into the sludge. His heavy burden made it impossible to stand. The more he struggled, the deeper he sank.

"This is *gross!*" Pliable yelled, arms flailing. "What is this even?!"

"It's... it's the Slough of Despond," Christian gasped, wiping grime from his face. "It's everything I regret. My guilt... my shame... my fear. It's all here, and I can't move."

"Well, I didn't sign up for this!" Pliable shouted. He clawed his way to the edge and scrambled out, dripping in mud. "Forget the City. I'm going back."

And just like that, Pliable was gone.

Christian stayed. Trapped. Exhausted. Doubting. But still wanting more.

He prayed. Cried out.

And just when he thought he'd sink for good—a hand reached out.

A man named Help pulled him out.

Soaked, shivering, but standing again, Christian whispered, "Thank you."

"Don't stop," Help said. "Keep walking. The path is still ahead."

Teen Commentary

The Mess That Almost Makes You Quit

Ever started something exciting—like seriously following Jesus—only to get hit with all your junk at once? The guilt, the doubt, the voice in your head saying, *"You'll never change"?*

That's the Slough of Despond.

It's messy. It's real. And it shows up early on the journey because healing usually starts with feeling all the stuff we've buried. The cool thing? Christian didn't climb out on his own—**someone came to help.** And that's the truth for us too. God doesn't expect us to clean ourselves up before we come to Him.

Also... let's talk about Pliable.

Some people will start the journey with you—but bail when it gets hard. That's not on you. Keep walking.

Reflection Questions

1. What "junk" weighs you down when you try to grow in your faith?

2. Have you ever felt like giving up spiritually because of how hard or messy it got?

3. Who's someone you could talk to when you're stuck in your own "Slough" moments?

4. How can you be a "Help" to someone else going through a dark time?

Scripture Connection

"He lifted me out of the slimy pit, out of the mud and mire; he set my feet on a rock and gave me a firm place to stand." —*Psalm 40:2 (NIV)*

Devotional Prayer

God, sometimes I feel stuck—overwhelmed by guilt, fear, or sadness. It's hard to move forward. But I know You're with me, even here. Please lift me out, remind me of Your love, and help me keep going.

In Jesus' Name, Amen.

MR. WORLDLY WISEMAN

Christian was still sore from the Slough—mud still crusted on his shoes and guilt still clinging to his heart like a second skin. He walked slowly, clutching the map the Evangelist had given him, determined to keep going toward the narrow gate.

That's when he saw him.

A well-dressed man with a perfect smile and polished shoes strolled up, walking like someone who'd never touched a puddle in his life.

"Good day, traveler," the man said smoothly. "You look troubled."

Christian sighed. "It's this burden. I can't get rid of it. I'm on my way to the narrow gate. That's where I was told I'd find relief."

The man raised a skeptical eyebrow. "Ah. One of *those* routes. Long, painful, unpopular. Dangerous, too. Look at you—you've already been through a swamp! There's a better way."

Christian hesitated. "A better way?"

"Absolutely," the man said with a grin. "Name's Mr. Worldly Wiseman. I know people. There's a town not far from here called Morality. Clean. Respectable. You'll meet a man named Legality— he'll tell you exactly what to do to fix yourself. No suffering required."

Christian's eyes lit up. "So I can get rid of this burden... without the hard stuff?"

Mr. Wiseman nodded. "Why struggle when you can *earn* your way back to peace?"

It sounded... smart. It sounded easier. Christian's feet turned toward the new path.

But the moment he stepped onto it, everything changed.

The road tilted steeply. Storm clouds rolled in. Thunder rumbled. Guilt slammed into him again like a crashing wave.

This wasn't peace. This was pressure.

He stumbled, overwhelmed, back onto the road he left. Just in time, Evangelist appeared again.

"Why did you listen to that man?" Evangelist asked, his voice gentle but firm. "Did I not tell you to go to the gate?"

Christian's head dropped. "He sounded right. I didn't want to suffer."

Evangelist looked him in the eye. "You don't earn peace, Christian. You receive it."

Teen Commentary

When the Shortcut Sounds Like Wisdom

Mr. Worldly Wiseman has smooth talk and shiny shoes. He's the voice that says, *"Just be a good person. Try harder. Fix yourself."* And honestly? That sounds great—until it crushes you.

Christian bought into the lie that he could clean himself up. A lot of us do. We think God will love us more if we follow the rules perfectly, or we try to hide our mess behind achievements, image, or even religion. But it doesn't work.

Jesus didn't come to patch us up—He came to rescue us.

And that shortcut? It's a trap.

Reflection Questions

1. Have you ever tried to "fix" your struggles or guilt on your own instead of going to God?

2. What "shortcut" voices are most tempting in your life—popularity, perfection, people-pleasing?

3. Why do you think it's hard to accept that salvation is a gift, not something you earn?

Scripture Connection

"God saved you by his grace when you believed. And you can't take credit for this; it is a gift from God. Salvation is not a reward for the good things we have done, so none of us can boast about it."—*Ephesians 2:8–9 (NLT)*

Devotional Prayer

Lord, it's so easy to listen to voices that offer comfort without truth. Help me not to trade what's right for what's easy. Keep me focused on Your path, even when it's hard. In Jesus' Name, Amen.

Scene 5

THE ONLY WAY

The Meeting with Evangelist

Christian stood frozen, caught off guard by the sudden voice behind him.

"Hey — what are you doing out here?" a calm, serious man asked. Christian didn't know how to answer at first. The words stuck in his throat.

The man stepped closer. "Aren't you the one I found crying just outside the City of Destruction?"

Christian swallowed hard. "Yes, that's me."

The man nodded knowingly. "Didn't I tell you to go to the little Wicket Gate?"

Christian hesitated, then answered, "Yes, sir."

"So how did you end up here, off the path?" the man asked.

Christian looked down, shame creeping over him. "After I got through the Slough of Despond, I met someone who said he could help me get rid of my burden. He said I didn't need to follow the hard path to the gate, that there was an easier way."

"And who was this man?" the other asked.

"He looked like a gentleman and talked convincingly. He told me he knew someone in the next village who could take off my burden. I believed him and turned away from the path. But when I reached this hill, and saw how dangerous it looked, I stopped. I didn't know what to do next."

Evangelist's voice was gentle but firm. "Show me your heart. Don't refuse to listen now."

Christian felt a chill run down his spine as the man began to read from a book.

"Don't ignore the one who speaks to you from heaven," Evangelist said, "because those who ignored the voice from earth didn't escape judgment. Now, the righteous live by faith — but anyone who turns back doesn't please God."

Christian's knees buckled. He fell to the ground, feeling hopeless. "Woe is me. I am ruined."

Evangelist reached out, helping him up. "You're forgiven if you believe. Don't give up now."

Christian shivered but stood again, trembling. Evangelist looked at him with steady eyes.

"Listen closely," he said. "The man who misled you is called Worldly Wiseman. He cares only about comfort and the ways of this world. He hates the cross and will do anything to avoid it."

Christian frowned, struggling to understand.

"There are three things about his advice you must hate: First, that he turned you off the true path — the path I sent you on, the path to the Wicket Gate. Second, that he made the cross look awful to you, as if it's something to avoid rather than something to embrace. Third, that he sent you to Legalism — a man who can't really help you, because he only knows rules and laws, which can never free you."

Christian's eyes widened. "Legalism? Is that the hill I saw? The one that seemed ready to fall on me?"

"Yes," said Evangelist. "Legalism is like Mount Sinai — scary, heavy, and impossible to climb. It's bondage, not freedom. No one is ever truly freed by following rules alone."

Christian looked away, ashamed. "I was a fool to listen to him."

Evangelist's voice softened. "You haven't lost everything. The gate is still open to you. But beware — don't turn off the path again. If you do, you might not get another chance."

Christian's heart pounded. "Can I still go back? Will they let me in? Or will I be sent away in shame?"

Evangelist smiled. "The man at the gate welcomes all who come, no matter how far they've wandered. But don't take his kindness for granted. Walk the narrow path, and don't look back."

Christian nodded, feeling a spark of hope for the first time in a long while.

Evangelist placed a hand on his shoulder and said, "Godspeed, my friend."

Christian turned back toward the Wicket Gate, ready to try again.

Teen Commentary

Why It's Okay to Mess Up — But Don't Stay There

Christian's story shows that even when we mess up and take the wrong path, it's not the end. It's easy to believe shortcuts or "easy fixes," especially when the right way looks tough or scary. But those shortcuts often lead to dead ends or more trouble.

What matters is being honest about where we are, facing the truth, and being brave enough to turn back and follow the right path again. God's grace means we can always start over — but the journey still demands courage, faith, and a willingness to keep going, even when it's hard.

Reflection Questions

1. Have you ever taken a "shortcut" in your faith or life, only to realize it didn't work? How did you respond?

2. What are some "Worldly Wisemen" voices you hear today that try to distract you from following God?

3. How does knowing God welcomes you back when you mess up encourage you to keep going?

Scripture Connection

"See to it that you do not refuse him who speaks. If they did not escape when they refused him who warned them on earth, how much less will we, if we turn away from him who warns us from heaven? ..." —*Hebrews 12:25-26 (NIV)*

Devotional Prayer

God, thank You for putting truth-speakers in my life who point me back to You. When I'm tempted to take shortcuts or stray from the path, remind me that Jesus is the only way. Help me trust You more than my own understanding. In Jesus' Name, Amen.

Scene 6

GOODWILL AT THE GATE

Christian's footsteps pounded the dirt path as he rushed forward, eyes fixed straight ahead. He didn't speak to anyone, not even when passersby called out to him. It felt like he was walking on thin ice—every step was shaky, and he couldn't shake the feeling that danger lurked just out of sight. The advice of Mr. Worldly Wiseman still echoed in his mind, but Christian knew deep down that it had led him off track.

Finally, Christian arrived at the gate. Above it, a simple sign was painted: **"Knock, and it will be opened for you."** His heart pounded. Taking a deep breath, he knocked—not once, but several times.

"Is it okay if I come in?" he called softly. "Will you open the door for someone like me—a sinner, a rebel who's made plenty of mistakes? If you do, I promise I'll sing your praise forever."

The gate creaked open, and a calm, serious man stepped out. His name was Goodwill.

"Who's there?" Goodwill asked, eyes kind but sharp.

Christian swallowed and answered, "It's me, a man weighed down by his mistakes. I'm from the city of Destruction, but I'm headed toward Mount Zion to be free from the wrath coming to my people. I've heard this gate leads there. Will you let me in?"

Without hesitation, Goodwill smiled and said, "Of course, with all my heart." Then he pushed the gate open wide.

Christian stepped forward—then suddenly felt a sharp tug on his sleeve.

"What was that for?" Christian asked, startled.

Goodwill's face grew serious. "Not far from here, there's a fortress ruled by Beelzebub. From there, he and his followers shoot arrows at anyone trying to reach this gate. They want to stop travelers from entering—sometimes even killing them."

Christian shivered. "I'm both scared and hopeful."

Once inside, Goodwill asked, "Who sent you here?"

"Evangelist," Christian replied. "He told me to come, knock, and that you'd tell me what to do next."

Goodwill nodded. "The door is open to you now—no one can close it."

Christian's chest swelled. "I'm starting to see that all the risk was worth it."

"But why did you come alone?" Goodwill asked.

"No one else saw the danger like I did," Christian said. "My wife and kids begged me to stay. Neighbors shouted for me to turn back. I plugged my ears and kept walking."

"Did anyone try to follow you?"

"Yes, two neighbors—Obstinate and Pliable. Obstinate gave up and went home angry. Pliable came with me a bit... until we fell into the Slough of Despond. He got scared and left, heading back toward home. So I continued alone."

Goodwill shook his head sadly. "Is heaven's glory so small that he won't risk a few challenges to reach it?"

Christian sighed. "That's true of Pliable—and honestly, of me too. I did turn aside for a while, listening to Mr. Worldly Wiseman's lies. He told me to find safety with Mr. Legality, but the mountain near his house almost crushed me. I barely escaped."

"That mountain has crushed many," Goodwill said gravely. "You were lucky to get away."

Christian nodded. "I don't know what would have happened if Evangelist hadn't found me again. It was God's mercy that brought me back."

Goodwill smiled gently. "We don't turn anyone away—no matter what they've done. Like the Bible says: 'All that the Father gives me will come to me, and whoever comes to me I will never drive away.'"

Christian felt relief wash over him.

"Now, come a little way with me," Goodwill said, stepping aside to show the path ahead. "See that narrow trail? That's the only way you should go. It's the path the patriarchs, prophets, Jesus, and the apostles walked—straight and true."

Christian frowned. "Are there no other paths that could lead me off track?"

"There are plenty," Goodwill warned. "Wide, crooked, confusing paths that seem easier. But only this narrow way leads to life."

Christian's eyes drifted to the heavy burden on his back. "Will you help me with this? I still carry it."

"Be patient," Goodwill said. "The burden will fall off when you reach the place of deliverance."

Christian squared his shoulders and prepared for the journey ahead.

"Further along, you'll find the house of the Interpreter," Goodwill said. "Knock there, and he'll show you things to help on your way."

Christian smiled for the first time in a long while. "Thank you, my friend."

"Go with Godspeed," Goodwill replied.

Teen Commentary

Hey, what just happened here? Christian's journey is a lot like starting something new that feels scary—like walking into a school you've never been to or trying out for a team. He's nervous, full of doubts, and carrying a heavy weight (kind of like guilt or worries we all have).

Goodwill is the friend who doesn't judge him, but is real about the risks. The narrow path? It's not always the easiest or most popular, but it's the right one. And even if others give up or try to distract you, you have to decide to keep moving forward.

Christian's story reminds us it's okay to be scared or mess up. What matters is that we don't give up, and we keep knocking on the right doors.

Reflection Questions

1. What "burdens" or worries are you carrying right now that feel heavy or hard to let go of?

2. Have you ever felt like Christian, where others around you don't see things the same way you do? How do you handle that?

3. What are some "wrong paths" that might seem easier but don't actually lead to what's best for you?

4. Who is someone like Goodwill in your life—a person who encourages you to keep going even when it's hard?

Scripture Connection

"Ask, and it will be given to you; seek, and you will find; knock, and the door will be opened to you." — *Matthew 7:7*

Devotional Prayer

Lord, thank You for welcoming me, even when I feel unworthy. Your grace opens the door I could never earn. Help me to trust Your love and keep moving forward, knowing I am always accepted in You. In Jesus' Name, Amen.

THE INTERPRETER'S HOUSE

Christian's boots crunched on the gravel as he walked toward the strange house at the edge of the path. He had been told to stop here, that someone inside would help him understand what lay ahead. The sky was gray and the wind tugged at his jacket as he knocked, again and again, on the heavy wooden door.

Finally, a woman peered through a crack. "Who's there?"

"Hi, I'm Christian," he said, trying to keep his voice steady. "A friend at the city gate said I should stop here. He said the master of this house could help me on my journey."

The door swung open, and an older man with kind eyes stepped out. "I'm the Interpreter. Come inside. There are things you need to see."

Christian followed him into a quiet room, where a soft candlelight flickered. The Interpreter motioned toward a painting hanging on the wall. It showed a serious man looking upward, holding a thick, worn book. His lips seemed to be speaking words, and behind him was a shadowy world he didn't notice. Above his head, a golden crown glimmered.

"What does this mean?" Christian asked, eyes locked on the picture.

"That man," the Interpreter said gently, "is someone who knows the truth and lives for something greater than this world. He spends his days pleading with others, teaching them to turn their eyes to heaven instead of being distracted by the things around them. His reward isn't here — it's in a world to come. He is your guide through the toughest parts of the journey."

Christian nodded, feeling something deep stirring inside him.

The Interpreter led him next into a dusty, neglected room. He called to a man nearby, who began sweeping — but the dust flew everywhere, choking Christian and blurring his vision. Then a girl brought a bucket of water, sprinkling it lightly. The dust settled, and the room suddenly felt fresh, even inviting.

"What's this?" Christian asked, coughing.

"The dust is sin, the dirt in a person's heart," the Interpreter explained. "The law is like the broom — it stirs things up, shows the mess, but can't clean it away. It makes you more aware of what's wrong but doesn't fix the problem. The water is the gospel — God's grace. It softens the dust, cleanses the heart, and makes everything pure again."

Christian thought about that. "So the law can make things worse, but the gospel brings real hope?"

"Exactly," said the Interpreter. "Don't forget it."

Then they entered a room where two boys sat on chairs. The older one, Passion, was fidgeting and restless, glaring at the other, Patience, who sat calmly, hands folded.

"Why does Passion look so upset?" Christian asked.

"The governor told them to wait for the best gifts until next year," said the Interpreter, "but Passion wants everything right now. Patience is willing to wait."

Just then, someone dropped a bag of treasure at Passion's feet. He grabbed it, smiled wildly, and laughed at Patience.

Christian watched as Passion wasted all the treasure quickly — and soon he was left with only rags.

"Tell me more," Christian said.

"Passion is like people who want all their happiness and pleasure right now, in this life. Patience waits for what's coming — the eternal reward. Passion's joy fades fast, but Patience will have glory that never ends."

Christian smiled. "Waiting is hard, but it's worth it."

The Interpreter nodded. "Exactly. Don't be fooled by quick thrills. The things we see now don't last. The things we can't see — like hope, peace, and God's kingdom — are forever."

Teen Commentary

Okay, so what just happened? Christian is on this huge, important journey, but he's not just walking blindly. The Interpreter shows him some *real* talk about life — like why trying to "clean up" your life with rules alone doesn't work, and why God's grace is the real deal for changing your heart.

Then there's Passion and Patience — two sides of how people handle life. Passion is the "I want it all now" kind of guy, chasing quick satisfaction and ignoring the long game. Patience, on the other hand, knows that waiting and trusting in God's promises pays off way more in the end. This is like when you want to binge-watch your favorite show all night but know you have a big test tomorrow. Waiting sucks, but it's worth it.

This story reminds us to focus on what really matters — not just the things we can see and get right away, but the eternal things God has for us if we stick with Him.

Reflection Questions

1. When have you felt like Passion — wanting everything right now? How did that work out?

2. What are some "dusty" things in your heart or life that rules alone can't fix?

3. How can you remind yourself to trust God's grace (the gospel) instead of just trying harder on your own?

4. What's one way you can practice patience and faith in something important this week?

Scripture Connection

"So we don't look at the troubles we can see now; rather, we fix our gaze on things that cannot be seen. For the things we see now will soon be gone, but the things we cannot see will last forever." —*2 Corinthians 4:18 (NLT)*

Devotional Prayer

Lord,
Open my eyes to see the truth You want to show me. Teach me through Your Word, and help me understand what really matters. Let the lessons I learn shape my heart and guide my path. In Jesus' Name, Amen.

Scene 8

THE CROSS

Christian ran hard, his breath coming in sharp bursts. The path stretched out in front of him, squeezed tight between two tall walls — walls that seemed to glow faintly with promise. On either side, the walls were labeled *Salvation*, like a fortress keeping him safe, but also reminding him how far he'd come and how far he still had to go.

His back ached under the weight of his burden — a heavy pack stuffed full of mistakes, regrets, and all the stuff he wished he could just throw away. Every step felt like a mountain, but he kept moving forward, driven by a hope he couldn't quite explain.

Then, the path tilted upward, and at the top stood a massive wooden Cross, rough and weathered. Below it, a dark cave-like tomb opened like a mouth waiting to swallow him whole.

Christian's heart pounded as he climbed the last few steps toward the Cross. Suddenly, he felt the weight on his back loosen. At first, just a little. Then, with a shocking *clunk*, the entire burden slipped off, tumbling down the hill like a rolling stone — straight into the tomb. It disappeared into the shadows, gone forever.

He stood there, stunned. His shoulders felt light — almost free. A strange warmth filled his chest, and tears welled up in his eyes. "He gave me rest by his pain… life by his death," Christian whispered, almost laughing through his tears.

He looked at the Cross, amazed. How could such a simple, rough thing bring such peace?

As he wiped his tears, three radiant figures appeared out of nowhere, shining like the sun. The first smiled and said, "Peace to you. Your sins are forgiven."

Christian's breath caught. Could it be true? Could he really start over?

The second stepped forward, peeling off Christian's tattered, dirty clothes and dressing him in fresh, bright clothes that fit perfectly. "You're clean now," the figure said. "No more shame."

The third marked a small sign on Christian's forehead — a seal that glowed softly. Then he handed Christian a sealed scroll and said, "Take this with you. It's your pass to the Celestial City. Hold it close."

Before Christian could say a word, the three angels vanished as quickly as they came. Christian jumped three times with joy, his voice bursting out in song as he sprinted down the path:

> "I came here weighed down by sin,
> Nothing helped until I reached this place.
> This is where the real journey starts —
> The burden's gone, the chains are snapped.
> Blessed Cross, blessed tomb, and blessed One who died for me!"

Teen Commentary

Okay, so picture this: You're carrying around all the stuff that drags you down — guilt, mistakes, all the "I'm not good enough" feelings. Christian's burden is like that heavy emotional backpack we all know too well.

But here's the game-changer: When he reaches the Cross, everything changes. His burden drops *off*, completely. That's not because he suddenly becomes perfect or stronger on his own — it's because someone else did the hard work for him. The Cross represents Jesus stepping in to take that weight away.

Then, Christian gets a fresh start: clean clothes (like a new identity), forgiveness, and a sealed promise that he belongs and is accepted. That seal? It's kind of like a VIP pass to God's eternal city.

This scene reminds us that real freedom comes when we stop trying to carry everything ourselves and trust Jesus to handle it. It's not just about feeling lighter — it's about being transformed from the inside out.

Reflection Questions

1. What are some burdens or worries you feel like you're carrying right now? How do they affect your daily life?

2. How does knowing that Jesus offers forgiveness and a fresh start change the way you see yourself?

3. What does it mean to you to have a "seal" or a mark that shows you belong to God?

4. Have you ever experienced a moment when you felt a real change inside, like Christian at the Cross? What brought that change?

Scripture Connection

"But he was pierced for our transgressions, he was crushed for our iniquities; the punishment that brought us peace was on him, and by his wounds we are healed." —*Isaiah 53:5*

Devotional Prayer

Jesus, thank You for carrying my sin to the cross. When I feel weighed down by guilt or shame, remind me that You already paid the price. Help me to live in the freedom and love You gave me there. In Your Name, Amen.

Scene 9

SIMPLE, SLOTH, AND PRESUMPTION

Christian walked down a quiet path, tired but determined. Then, off to the side, he noticed something strange — three guys slumped against a rock, completely out cold. Their feet were chained, but they didn't seem to care.

Christian edged closer and saw their names written on little signs hanging around their necks: *Simple*, *Sloth*, and *Presumption*.

"Hey!" Christian said, shaking Simple's shoulder. "Wake up! You're sleeping on the edge of a cliff, and below you is a bottomless pit. You're in serious trouble if you stay here."

Simple barely opened his eyes. "Nah, I don't see any danger," he mumbled, then closed them again.

Christian turned to Sloth, who yawned and stretched like he just wanted five more minutes. "Come on, man! If you keep this up, you're going to fall. You can't afford to snooze your life away."

Sloth rubbed his eyes. "Just a little more sleep…" he whispered, drifting back.

Christian's voice got firmer as he faced Presumption. "You think you can just stand here on your own, without help? That's a mistake. Danger is coming — like a hungry lion looking for a meal. You need to wake up and get out of these chains."

Presumption grinned arrogantly. "Every vat stands on its own bottom," he said, meaning he thought he could handle it alone.

Christian shook his head, frustration building. "You're all making the same mistake. Wake up before it's too late!" But the three just settled back down, their eyes closing for good this time.

Christian sighed, feeling the weight of their choice, and kept moving forward alone.

Teen Commentary

So, what's going on here? Christian meets three guys who are basically trapped — not by chains you can see every day, but by chains they don't want to break free from: ignorance (Simple), laziness (Sloth), and thinking they can handle everything alone (Presumption).

Think about your own life. Sometimes we get stuck because we ignore problems, procrastinate, or assume everything will just work out without help. It's like we're snoozing through important stuff or acting like we're invincible.

Christian tries to wake them up because he knows danger is real — temptation, bad choices, and consequences can catch up fast if you're not paying attention.

The hard truth? You can't grow or move forward if you're chained to denial, laziness, or pride. But the good news is, it's *possible* to break free if you're willing to wake up and ask for help.

Reflection Questions

1. What are some "chains" or habits that might be holding you back right now?

2. Have you ever ignored a warning or procrastinated on something important? How did that work out?

3. Why do you think it's so hard to admit we need help sometimes?

4. What can you do today to start "waking up" from anything that's keeping you stuck?

Scripture Connection

"Be alert and of sober mind. Your enemy the devil prowls around like a roaring lion looking for someone to devour." —*1 Peter 5:8*

Devotional Prayer

God, sometimes I act like I've got all the time in the world or like I can handle life on my own. Wake me up when I start drifting, and break any chains that are holding me back — whether it's laziness, pride, or ignoring what You're trying to tell me. Help me stay alert and ready to follow You. In Jesus' Name, Amen.

Scene 10

FORMALIST AND HYPOCRISY

Christian was walking along the narrow path, feeling the weight of the journey ahead. Suddenly, he noticed two guys tumbling clumsily over a wall beside the trail. They dusted themselves off and hurried over to him. Christian recognized them immediately: one was *Formalist* and the other *Hypocrisy*.

"Hey, where are you two coming from? And what's your destination?" Christian asked, raising an eyebrow.

"We're from Vain-glory," Formalist said with a proud grin. "And we're headed for Mount Zion — the place everyone wants to be praised and admired."

Christian frowned. "That's great, but why didn't you come in through the gate at the start of the path? Don't you know it's written that anyone who climbs in over the wall is a thief and a robber?"

Formalist scoffed. "The gate's too far out of the way. Besides, everyone back home takes the shortcut—climbing the wall is just how it's done. We've been doing it for over a thousand years, and no one's complained."

Hypocrisy nodded confidently. "Yeah, if we're in the right path, does it matter how we got here? You walked in the proper way, but we're in the way, too. So what's the difference?"

Christian shook his head slowly, trying to keep his voice calm. "I'm following the rule of my Master — the one who made this path. You're just following whatever feels right to you. The Lord who owns this city counts you as thieves, because you came without His permission. That means you won't be welcomed at the end."

The two exchanged smug looks. "Well, you better watch yourself," Formalist said, "we follow all the laws and traditions just as carefully as you do."

Christian looked them both in the eye. "You think following rules is enough? That's not how it works. You won't be saved by ticking boxes if you didn't come through the gate — through the right way. My coat," he pointed to the simple garment he wore, "was given to me by the Lord of this city. It's a gift to cover my shame. And this mark on my forehead?" Christian touched his temple. "It was put there by one of His closest friends when I was set free from my burden. Plus, I have this roll," he pulled out a small, sealed scroll, "a promise from the Lord that I'll be allowed in."

Formalist and Hypocrisy just laughed and walked away, leaving Christian alone again. He sighed deeply but didn't lose hope. He read his roll and felt its words refresh his spirit as he reached the foot of a steep hill named Difficulty.

There were three paths here: one straight up the hill, and two others turning off to the sides. Christian knelt and drank from a fresh spring at the base, feeling new strength.

He smiled and whispered, "This hill is tough, but the right path is worth the struggle. Better to go hard and true than easy and wrong."

Formalist and Hypocrisy paused at the hill, looking up at the steep climb. They shrugged and chose the side paths — one called Danger, leading into a dark forest, and the other named Destruction, into a shadowy valley. Christian watched them go, knowing their choices would not end well.

Teen Commentary

Alright, here's the deal — Christian is on a serious journey, and he's all about doing things *the right way*, even if it's hard. But Formalist and Hypocrisy? They want the *look* of being good, the praise, and to get there without the effort or truth.

Sounds familiar? Sometimes in life, people take shortcuts or pretend to be better than they are — showing off what's on the outside while missing the real heart work. Formalist follows "rules" but misses the point, while Hypocrisy pretends to be genuine but hides the truth.

Christian's "coat" and "mark" aren't just clothes — they represent God's gift of forgiveness and identity. He trusts in God's grace, not just his own effort or pretending.

The big question: Are you okay with the hard path of honesty, growth, and faith — or are you tempted to take shortcuts and fake it?

Reflection Questions

1. Can you think of a time when you or someone else took a "shortcut" instead of doing the hard but right thing? What happened?

2. How do you feel when people act one way on the outside but are very different inside? Have you ever done that?

3. What does it mean to you that Christian's coat and mark were given by someone else — not earned by himself?

4. What are some "paths" in your life where you need courage to choose the harder but better way?

Scripture Connection

"We know that a person is not justified by the works of the law, but by faith in Jesus Christ. So we, too, have put our faith in Christ Jesus that we may be justified by faith in Christ and not by the works of the law, because by the works of the law no one will be justified." — *Galatians 2:16*

Devotional Prayer

God, I don't want to fake my faith or try to impress people by just looking good on the outside. Help me follow You the real way — through faith in Jesus, not through shortcuts or pretending. Give me courage to take the harder path when it's right, and to live with honesty, humility, and grace. In Jesus' Name, Amen.

Scene 11

TIMOROUS AND MISTRUST

C hristian pushed himself up the steep hill, breath coming in sharp gasps. His legs shook, and soon he was no longer walking — he was crawling, hands and knees scraping the rough ground. The hill was tougher than he expected, but he was determined to keep going.

About halfway up, he spotted a small wooden shelter nestled under a cluster of trees—a cozy little hideout that looked like it was made just for tired travelers. Christian crawled over and collapsed inside, relief flooding through him as he sank onto the bench.

He pulled out his roll—the small, worn scroll tucked inside his jacket—and read the words again. The promises written there warmed his heart. He looked down at the simple coat he wore, the one given to him at the cross, and smiled. It was like a shield, reminding him he wasn't alone.

His eyelids grew heavy. Just for a moment, he thought… and then he drifted off. Deep sleep pulled him under, and the roll slipped from his hand onto the floor.

Suddenly, a voice broke through the quiet. "Hey, wake up! Go watch the ants, lazybones. Learn from them."

Christian jolted upright, startled awake by the stranger's words. The voice stuck with him: *"Go to the ant, thou sluggard; consider her ways, and be wise."*

Shaking off the last of his sleep, Christian grabbed his roll and pushed himself up. He sped up the rest of the hill, heart pounding and spirit recharged.

At the very top, just as he caught his breath, two guys came barreling toward him — panic written all over their faces. One was called Timorous, the other Mistrust.

Christian raised his hand to stop them. "Hey! You're running the wrong way! What's going on?"

Timorous gulped. "We started toward the City of Zion, but the higher we climb, the scarier it gets. We're turning back. It's just too dangerous."

Mistrust nodded rapidly. "Yeah, and there are lions up ahead. We don't know if they're asleep or awake, but if they catch us, we're done for."

Christian's heart skipped a beat. Fear crept into his chest like a shadow. "You're scaring me... But where could I run to? If I go back, it's my old home—fire, brimstone, and death for sure. If I keep going, it's scary, but it leads to life. I have to choose. Going back means death, but moving forward means risking fear for hope. I'll keep going."

With that, Christian tightened his grip on his roll and started down the steep path, choosing courage over fear.

Teen Commentary

Facing Fear and Doubt on the Hard Path

You know that moment when you're trying something new or tough, and suddenly all the "what ifs" start screaming in your head? That's exactly what Timorous and Mistrust are dealing with — they're scared, doubting, and want to run back to what's comfortable, even if it's dangerous.

Christian? He's scared too. But he remembers what's waiting for him at the top — safety, hope, a place where fear and danger don't win. His secret weapons? The promises from his roll (God's Word) and the courage to keep going, even when the path gets rough.

Fear is real and natural. But it doesn't have to stop you. What if you let your hope be louder than your fear?

Reflection Questions

1. When have you felt like Timorous or Mistrust—ready to quit because things got too scary? What helped you keep going?

2. What are some "lions" in your life that make you afraid? How could you face them with courage?

3. How can God's promises (like the ones Christian reads in his roll) give you strength when you feel weak or scared?

4. What does it look like to choose hope over fear in your everyday life?

Scripture Connection

"Go to the ant, you sluggard; consider its ways and be wise." — *Proverbs 6:6*

Devotional Prayer

God, sometimes fear and doubt hit me hard, and I just want to run back to what feels safe—even if it's not good for me. Help me to trust You when the road gets scary. Remind me of Your promises and give me courage to keep moving forward, even when I'm afraid. Let hope be louder than fear in my heart. In Jesus' Name, Amen.

Scene 12

SLEEP IN THE DAYTIME

Christian kept walking, but his steps weren't confident anymore. The words of Timorous and Mistrust replayed in his mind like a broken song. Fear crept in again. He reached for his scroll—the one that always gave him comfort when he felt like giving up.

His heart stopped. It wasn't there.

He patted his jacket, checked his bag. Nothing.

Panic punched him in the chest. That scroll wasn't just comforting words—it was proof he was on the right path, his "pass" into the Celestial City. Without it, everything felt shaky.

He closed his eyes, heart racing. *Where did I last see it?*

Then it hit him—the nap. Back at the little rest stop halfway up the hill. He had fallen asleep. He wasn't supposed to stay there long… and now he had lost what mattered most.

Christian sank to his knees on the trail. "God, I messed up. Please forgive me," he whispered.

Wiping his eyes, he turned around and began the climb *back down*—retracing his steps, scanning every bush and stone with the ache of regret growing heavier. He sighed. He groaned. He even scolded himself out loud.

"Why did I fall asleep during the day? In the middle of the climb?" he muttered. "That rest was for renewal—not laziness. I've lost time. I've lost progress. And now I'll probably lose daylight too."

When he finally reached the rest stop, it felt like a gut punch. Just seeing it brought all the shame rushing back. But he didn't stop searching. He got on his knees, checked under the bench—

There it was.

His scroll. Right where he had dropped it. He snatched it up with trembling hands and hugged it close to his chest. His eyes welled up again—this time not with grief, but with gratitude.

"Thank You, God," he whispered through happy tears.

Refreshed by forgiveness and fueled by grace, Christian stood and began climbing the hill again—faster than before, heart lighter. But the sun was dipping below the horizon. He had wasted precious time.

"Oh, that I hadn't fallen asleep," he said. "Now I might have to walk in the dark, right into danger."

As the shadows stretched across the trail, he remembered what Mistrust and Timorous said—about lions. They hunt at night. What if they were still out there?

Then, just ahead, something broke through the gloom: a shining building, tall and strong, standing right next to the path.

A palace.

A place called *Beautiful.*

Teen Commentary

Don't Sleep Through Your Moment

This scene hits hard.

Christian didn't do something *wildly wrong*. He just... got comfortable. Took a nap. Delayed a little. Let down his guard.

That's way too easy to do in real life, right? Maybe it's procrastinating when you know God's calling you to grow. Or maybe it's becoming spiritually "asleep"—just going through the motions, losing your sense of urgency. Christian paid the price: lost time, lost momentum, and walking into danger when he could've been walking in the light.

But the best part? God didn't leave him lost. When he turned around, God helped him find what he lost. Grace picked him up again.

This scene reminds us that it's okay to admit when we've gotten off track—as long as we *get back up*. Your "scroll" might be your faith, your joy, your sense of purpose. If you've lost it, don't stay stuck. Go back. Repent. And get moving again.

The Palace Beautiful is just ahead.

Reflection Questions

1. Have you ever felt like you've "fallen asleep" in your faith—become lazy, distracted, or spiritually numb? What woke you up?

2. What "scroll" (truth, promise, calling) have you lost sight of that you need to recover?

3. How do you balance rest and renewal with the urgency of your spiritual journey?

4. What does it look like to keep going—even after a mistake or setback?

Scripture Connection

"So then, let us not be like others, who are asleep, but let us be awake and sober. For those who sleep, sleep at night... But since we belong to the day, let us be sober, putting on faith and love as a breastplate, and the hope of salvation as a helmet." —*1 Thessalonians 5:6-8 (NIV)*

Devotional Prayer

Father, sometimes I get tired and lose my focus. I drift away from what's most important, and I lose my way. Forgive me for the times I've let my faith grow sleepy or distracted. Help me to find what I've lost—your promises, your strength—and get back on the right path. Give me the courage to keep going, even when I've made mistakes. Thank You for never giving up on me. In Jesus' Name, Amen.

Scene 13

ENTERING THE PALACE "BEAUTIFUL"

Christian jogged up the dusty path, heart racing and backpack bouncing against his shoulders. The setting sun painted everything gold, and all he could think about was getting to that safe-looking house on the hill. It stood tall, like a beacon of hope, with a warm glow in the windows. He picked up his pace.

But then—he froze.

The path narrowed sharply, funneling him into a rocky corridor, and there, in the fading light, he spotted them.

Two lions.

Massive. Muscles rippling. Eyes locked on him like he was dinner.

Christian's breath caught in his throat. His backpack slipped from his hand. *This is what Mistrust and Timorous were talking about*, he realized. *This is why they turned back.*

His feet itched to run.

But just as he began to step back, a voice called out from a nearby guardhouse.

"Is your strength really that small?" It was a man in a simple uniform, standing by the door of the house on the hill. "Don't be afraid of the lions—they're chained. They're only here to test who's got real faith. Stay in the center of the path and you'll be fine!"

Christian squinted. Sure enough, he saw the thick chains anchoring the lions to either side. They couldn't reach the middle. He took a shaky breath, his heart pounding so hard it hurt.

"Okay… okay…" he whispered to himself. "Just walk. Just don't look them in the eyes."

The lions roared as he passed. He flinched but stayed in the middle, each step fueled by fear and faith clashing inside him. When he finally reached the gate, his knees almost buckled with relief.

"Sir," he said to the gatekeeper, "what is this place? Can I stay here tonight?"

The man smiled. "This is the House Beautiful. It was built by the King himself—for travelers like you who are weary from the journey. What's your name?"

"I used to be called Graceless," Christian said, "but now my name is Christian. I'm headed to Zion, but I got delayed. I… I fell asleep back there and lost my proof. I had to go back and find it."

The gatekeeper nodded with compassion. "We all stumble. I'll call someone to meet you."

He rang a small bell, and a graceful young woman named Discretion stepped out. She asked Christian some questions—where he came from, what he'd seen, why he was on this journey. As he spoke, she listened carefully, her eyes softening with every word.

When he finished, she smiled, tears brimming. "Wait here," she said, disappearing inside.

A moment later, three other young women appeared—Piety, Prudence, and Charity. They welcomed Christian with warm eyes and open arms.

"Come in, blessed traveler," Charity said. "This house was made just for people like you."

Christian bowed his head, overwhelmed by kindness. He stepped inside, the door closing behind him. They handed him a cup of cool water, and for the first time in a long time, he felt safe.

Teen Commentary

Facing Your Lions

You ever been *this* close to something good, something you've worked for—only to get stopped cold by fear? That's Christian in this scene. He's exhausted, scared, and ready to turn back *right when he's about to find rest*. Sound familiar?

Sometimes fear looks like anxiety before a big decision. Or doubt when you've finally taken a step of faith. Or temptation, pushing you to give up because "it's too much." But here's the truth: some of the scariest things standing in your way are *chained*. Fear can roar, but it can't destroy you if you walk in faith and stay on the path.

The palace—"Beautiful"—is like Christian community. It's where you're known, refreshed, and reminded of truth. But first? You've gotta push past the roar.

Reflection Questions

1. What "lions" (fears or challenges) are standing in the way of your next step of faith right now?

2. Have you ever turned back from something you knew God was leading you to because it looked too scary?

3. What does it mean to "stay in the middle of the path" in your own walk with God?

4. Who in your life is like Watchful or Discretion—someone who helps you see clearly when you're scared or confused?

Scripture Connection

"For the Spirit God gave us does not make us timid, but gives us power, love and self-discipline." —*2 Timothy 1:7 (NIV)*

Devotional Prayer

Lord, sometimes fear feels so real and strong—like lions blocking my way. Help me to remember that You've chained those fears and that I don't have to turn back. Give me the courage to keep walking in faith, staying on the path You've set. Thank You for the safe places and people You send to encourage me when I'm weary. Help me to trust You more than my fears. In Jesus' Name, Amen.

Scene 14

PIETY

Christian sat cross-legged on a soft rug near the fire, the warmth easing the stiffness in his legs. Across from him sat three young women—Piety, Prudence, and Charity—each with kind eyes and a gentle presence. They weren't just curious. They cared.

"So," Piety leaned forward, elbows on her knees, "you've come a long way, Christian. Would you mind telling us what's brought you here?"

Christian nodded, grateful for the chance to finally breathe and share. "Yeah... honestly, it started with this overwhelming sense that if I didn't get out of where I was, I'd be lost forever. It was like this voice echoing in my mind, warning me about destruction. I couldn't ignore it anymore."

Piety's eyes softened. "And how did you know where to go?"

"I didn't," Christian admitted with a short laugh. "I was scared and completely lost. But then, out of nowhere, this man named Evangelist showed up. He found me crying and confused and pointed me toward a gate—he called it the 'Wicket Gate.' I never would've seen it on my own."

"Did you stop at the Interpreter's house along the way?" Prudence asked.

Christian lit up. "Yes! That place changed me. I saw some intense stuff—like this picture of Jesus holding onto someone's heart, even while Satan was throwing everything at him to take it. It showed me how much grace is at work even when I mess up."

He paused, then continued, more quietly. "There was also this guy who had totally given up on God. He believed he'd sinned too far to ever be forgiven. That scared me because I realized how easy it would be to fall into that lie."

"What else?" Charity asked gently.

"There was a dream…" Christian said, looking into the fire. "A man thought the Day of Judgment had come, and he hadn't prepared. He woke up screaming. It shook me. I knew I didn't want to live unprepared anymore."

They were quiet for a moment. Then Piety asked, "Was there anything else that left a mark on you?"

Christian smiled, eyes watering just a little. "Yeah. The Cross. I saw someone—Jesus—bleeding, hanging there. And when I looked at Him… the weight I was carrying on my back just… fell. I had carried that burden for so long, I thought I'd never be free."

The girls leaned in, listening with reverence.

"Then three shining people came. One said my sins were forgiven. Another gave me this coat"—he pulled at the hem of the embroidered tunic he now wore—"and the third marked my forehead and gave me this scroll." He took a sealed roll out of his jacket. "Proof of the promise."

"Christian," Piety said gently, "you've seen so much already. Anything else?"

He nodded slowly. "I saw people sleeping on the side of the path—Simple, Sloth, and Presumption. I tried to wake them, but they wouldn't move. Then there were Formalist and Hypocrisy, who thought they could sneak into the journey without going through the gate. They didn't make it far."

He looked down. "The hardest part was climbing the Hill Difficulty and passing the lions. I almost turned around. But then the porter—Watchful—called out and told me to stay on the path. If he hadn't…"

He trailed off, then looked up at the three with genuine gratitude. "But now I'm here. And I'm thankful God led me safely. And I'm thankful for you all, too. Thank you for letting me in."

Teen Commentary

Ever been asked to tell your story? Christian's doing that here. He's reflecting on how far he's come—and let's be real, it wasn't easy. From fear of destruction to the Cross that set him free, his journey's packed with moments that a lot of us can relate to:

- Feeling weighed down by guilt or shame

- Not knowing where to go or what to do

- Almost giving up because the obstacles feel too huge

- Meeting people (like Evangelist or Watchful) who speak truth when we need it most

What's powerful here is how Christian *remembers* every moment. He's not rushing past the pain or skipping the scary parts. He's being honest about them—and that's what makes his faith real.

Maybe you haven't seen "lions" or glowing angels, but you've probably faced moments of fear, guilt, or doubt. And just like Christian, you're not alone.

Reflection Questions

1. Have you ever felt like you were carrying a heavy burden (guilt, shame, fear)? What helped you let it go—or what's still weighing you down?

2. Who has been like Evangelist in your life—someone who pointed you in the right direction when you were lost?

3. What's one "scene" from your life that still sticks with you and reminds you of God's faithfulness?

4. Why do you think it's important to look back and remember your journey with God?

Scripture Connection

"Come to me, all you who are weary and burdened, and I will give you rest." — *Matthew 11:28 (NIV)*

Devotional Prayer

Father, thank You for being with me on this journey. Thank You for lifting my burdens and sending people to help me when I felt lost. Help me remember how far You've brought me and trust You with what's ahead. Give me rest, courage, and a heart that stays close to You. In Jesus' Name, Amen.

Scene 15

PRUDENCE

The cozy room glowed with a soft light as the fire crackled in the hearth. Christian sat in a well-worn armchair, cradling a warm mug of tea between his hands. Across from him sat Prudence—a thoughtful, kind-eyed young woman with a calm presence that made you want to spill your whole story without even being asked.

"So," Prudence said, leaning forward slightly, "do you ever think about the place you came from?"

Christian's expression shifted. "Yeah… I do," he admitted. "But when I think about it, it's not with longing—it's with regret. I was living in a place that was slowly destroying me, and I didn't even realize it at first. If I kept thinking fondly about it, I'd probably turn around and go back. But honestly? I don't want that life. I want something better—something *eternal*. That's why I left. I'm chasing after a better country—a heavenly one."

Prudence nodded slowly. "But… do you ever feel like the old habits and thoughts from back there still cling to you?"

Christian let out a long sigh. "More than I'd like to admit. It's like I'm dragging chains I didn't even know were still attached. My old way of thinking—it creeps back in, even when I don't want it to. Sometimes it's pride. Other times it's temptation, or fear, or just wanting to give up. And even though I hate those thoughts now…

they still show up. I wish I could forget all of it for good. But the fight is real."

"That sounds exhausting," Prudence said gently. "But are there times when it feels like you've actually won that fight?"

Christian's face softened. "Yeah. But those moments are rare—like glimpses of sunlight on a cloudy day. I treasure them. They keep me going."

"Do you know what helps in those moments?" she asked.

He smiled. "I think about the cross. What I saw there changed everything. When I remember what Jesus did for me, it quiets the storm inside. Or I'll touch the scroll He gave me—that reminder of His promise. And this coat He gave me—it replaced my old rags. Just thinking about where I'm headed... that's enough to lift me out of the dark."

Prudence's voice was warm. "So why are you so eager to reach Mount Zion?"

Christian's eyes lit up. "Because that's where I'll finally see Him face-to-face—the one who died for me. And I'll finally be free of all the stuff I still struggle with. No more shame. No more inner war. Just peace. And I'll be with people who get it—people who've walked the same road, who love Him like I do. I'll be home. And I'll never have to cry or hurt again. That's what I want."

Teen Commentary

Still Struggling? Same.

Let's be real. Christian might've left his old life behind, but that *doesn't mean the struggle left him*. And honestly? That's *super relatable*. Maybe you've tried to move on from stuff—habits, relationships, thoughts—but those things still pop up like ads you didn't ask for.

Here's the deal: You're not alone. Even when you've given your life to Jesus, the battle inside doesn't magically disappear. But like Christian, we fight with hope. Not fake "smile-through-it" vibes, but real, raw hope that looks to the cross and remembers—*Jesus already won*.

And those moments where things feel light and free? Treasure them. They're reminders that you're not fighting in vain. You're headed somewhere. And the God who saved you isn't ashamed of you—He's preparing a place for you.

Reflection Questions

1. What "old country" thoughts or habits try to pull you back? How do you respond?

2. Have you ever had a "golden hour" moment when you felt free from guilt or temptation? What helped bring that about?

3. Why do you think God allows us to struggle instead of just removing our temptations completely?

4. What motivates you to keep moving forward in your faith when the road gets hard?

Scripture Connection

"For I do not do the good I want to do, but the evil I do not want to do—this I keep on doing... What a wretched man I am! Who will rescue me from this body that is subject to death? Thanks be to God, who delivers me through Jesus Christ our Lord!"— *Romans 7:19, 24–25 (NIV)*

Devotional Prayer

Lord, You know the battles I still face—the old thoughts, the old habits. Thank You for not giving up on me. Remind me of the Cross when I feel weak, and keep my heart focused on the hope ahead. Help me walk in freedom, one step at a time. In Jesus' Name, Amen.

Scene 16

CHARITY

Charity leaned forward, her eyes kind but searching. She was probably in her early twenties, calm but clearly deep-thinking. She'd been watching Christian quietly for a while now. "Can I ask you something personal?" she said.

Christian nodded, shoulders a little tense.

"Do you have a family? Like… are you married?"

His face softened instantly, the pain hitting like a sudden storm. "Yeah," he said quietly. "I've got a wife. And four little kids."

Her eyebrows rose. "Wait—then why are you here alone? Why didn't they come with you on this journey?"

Christian looked down, swallowed hard, then his voice cracked. "I wanted them to come. I begged them to. But they didn't want to. They thought I'd lost it, that all this about destruction and judgment was nonsense. I pleaded, but it was like talking to a wall."

Charity tilted her head, sympathy rising in her voice. "Did you explain to them how serious it was? How dangerous it is to stay behind?"

"I did," he said, rubbing his face. "Over and over. I told them what God showed me—that our city was doomed. But they laughed. Thought I was just being dramatic. Like I was trying to scare them."

Charity nodded solemnly. "That had to hurt. Did you at least pray for them?"

"I did. Every night. I still do. I love them with everything in me. That's what makes this so hard."

She leaned back a bit, thinking. "Did you tell them what it was doing to *you*? Like how much it broke you inside?"

"I tried," Christian whispered. "I cried in front of them. I couldn't hide it—my fear, my anxiety. They saw how much it wrecked me to think of what was coming. But it didn't change anything. They still refused."

"And… did they give a reason? Why they wouldn't come?"

He let out a sad laugh. "My wife… she didn't want to give up the life she had. She was afraid of losing comfort, money, security. And the kids? They were just… into stuff. Games. Friends. Fun. They didn't want to leave all that behind."

Charity nodded, gently. "Sometimes people see truth in your words, but if your actions don't match, it can push them away. Do you think how you lived your life before might've hurt your message?"

Christian didn't flinch. "I won't pretend I was perfect. I messed up, plenty. But when I realized the truth, I tried to live differently. I avoided anything that might trip them up or make them think I was fake. But even that made them mad—they said I was being 'too extreme,' like I thought I was better than them just because I wouldn't do what they were doing."

Charity sighed. "That's actually common. Cain hated Abel because Abel did what was right—it made Cain's choices look worse. Maybe your family was reacting like that too. But listen: you told them the truth. You warned them. You loved them. You prayed. You lived carefully. Their choices aren't on you anymore."

Christian's eyes shimmered with tears again. "I hope you're right."

"I am," she said firmly. "You've done what you could. Now keep going. You're not walking alone."

Teen Commentary

Ugh. Isn't it the *worst* when you care so much about someone—family, friends, teammates—but they just *don't get it?*

Christian's heartbreak is something a lot of teens know. You're trying to follow Jesus. You've seen how real He is. But when you try to share it, the people you love might roll their eyes or say, *"You've changed, and not in a good way."* It's frustrating. Painful. And it can make you feel really alone.

But here's the key: Christian didn't give up. He wept. He prayed. He lived it out. And he trusted that even if his family didn't come now, his job was still to follow the path.

And so is yours.

Jesus gets it. Remember, *His own family* thought He was crazy once (Mark 3:21). You're in good company.

Reflection Questions

1. Have you ever felt like Christian—wanting someone to come closer to God, but they just won't listen?

2. How can you live in a way that shows Jesus is real—without coming across as "better than" others?

3. What's one way you can pray for someone you love who's not walking with God?

4. How do you keep going in faith when people closest to you don't understand?

Scripture Connection

"But if you warn the wicked person and they do not turn from their wickedness or from their evil ways, they will die for their sin; but you will have saved yourself."— *Ezekiel 3:19 (NIV)*

Devotional Prayer

Lord, You know how much it hurts when the people I love don't understand my faith. I've tried, I've prayed, I've wept—and still, they don't come. Give me peace to trust You with their hearts, and strength to keep walking with You even when I feel alone. Help me love without giving up, and live in a way that points them to You. In Jesus' Name, Amen.

Scene 17

THE LORD OF THE HILL

Christian sat at a long wooden table, the fire crackling nearby as evening wrapped the house in golden warmth. The place felt like a safehouse for the soul. Around him were a few others—faithful pilgrims like him—who had been through their own storms but were still holding on.

The kitchen door swung open and a woman named Mercy carried in a tray of food that smelled like it had been seasoned in heaven itself. Roast meat, soft bread, fruit bursting with color, and glasses filled with sparkling, refined wine. Christian's stomach growled, but his heart was fuller than his plate. This was more than dinner. It was belonging.

They bowed their heads in thanks, and as they began to eat, their conversation naturally turned to *Him*—the Lord of the Hill.

"Did you know," said one pilgrim, slicing into his food, "that He didn't just build this place for rest—He fought for it. Fought *for us.*"

Christian leaned in, eyes wide. "I've heard," he said quietly. "They say He went into battle against the one who holds the power of death itself."

"The devil," someone confirmed. "And He won. But it cost Him everything."

Christian's grip tightened on his cup. "His own blood."

"He didn't have to do it," added Mercy. "But He *wanted* to. That's the crazy part. All out of love for us—ordinary people. He gave up everything so we wouldn't have to live in fear, chained to death anymore."

"And get this," another voice chimed in, "some people here *met* Him. After He died."

Christian blinked. "Wait, *after?*"

"Yep," the young man said. "He's alive. They heard it from His own mouth: He *loves* pilgrims like us. Like, truly loves us."

Christian leaned back in awe. "I've never known love like that."

"And He's not just saving people," Mercy added, "He's lifting them up. Taking nobodies—beggars, outsiders—and making them royalty. *Princes.* Like, *we're* being made into that."

Christian sat in stunned silence, letting the words wash over him. He thought of where he started—broken, alone, desperate—and where he now sat: full, safe, surrounded by others, talking about a Savior who died so that people like *him* could be rescued.

That night, after more stories and grateful laughter, they prayed together and headed to their rooms. Christian was given a spacious upper room called *Peace*. He climbed into the bed near a window that looked out to the east. As dawn crept across the sky, painting it in soft pinks and golds, Christian awoke and whispered:

"Where even *am* I? This love… this care… that Jesus would welcome a broken guy like me? It's like I'm already at the edge of heaven."

Teen Commentary

You're Not Just a Guest—You're Family

This scene hits *different*. Imagine being Christian. You're tired, worn out from the journey, and then—boom—you're wrapped in warmth, safety, and surrounded by people who *get it*. But even more, they start talking about *Him*—the One who made it all possible.

This Lord of the Hill isn't just some distant CEO-God. He's a warrior. A rescuer. A *sacrifice*. He gave everything because He *wanted* you. And not because you're already awesome, but because His love *makes* you valuable. He raises *beggars into royalty*. That includes you.

If you've ever felt like you don't belong, or like your past disqualifies you from anything good—this scene is a reminder: Jesus didn't wait for you to fix yourself. He came down and bled for you, fought for you, and *still* loves you, right where you are.

You're not just on a journey. You're being adopted. Raised. Honored.

Reflection Questions

1. How does knowing that Jesus fought and died for you—*personally*—change how you see yourself?

2. What part of Christian's experience in the house of peace speaks most to where you are right now?

3. Why do you think it's hard for some people to believe that God wants to lift *them* up?

4. If Jesus really loves you this deeply, what's one way you can respond this week?

Scripture Connection

"Since the children have flesh and blood, He too shared in their humanity so that by His death He might break the power of him who holds the power of death—that is, the devil—and free those who all their lives were held in slavery by their fear of death."—*Hebrews 2:14–15 (NIV)*

Devotional Prayer

Jesus, thank You for fighting for me, for loving me when I was broken and far away. You didn't wait for me to be worthy—you made me worthy. Help me rest in Your love, live like someone You've rescued, and remember I'm not just a guest in Your house—I'm family. Amen.

Scene 18

THE RARITIES OF "BEAUTIFUL"

Christian blinked as soft morning light poured through the window of his room called *Peace*. The sunrise painted the sky in gold and rose, and for the first time in a long while, he felt fully rested—body and soul.

After breakfast, one of the hosts approached with a gentle smile. "Before you go," she said, "there are some things we want to show you. This place isn't called *Beautiful* for nothing."

Intrigued, Christian followed her down a long hallway into a large study with shelves stacked from floor to ceiling. The room felt ancient and alive, like history had a heartbeat.

"This," she said, handing him an old, weathered scroll, "is the story of the Lord of the Hill. His lineage traces back to the Ancient of Days. He wasn't just born—He *always* was."

Christian's eyes scanned the words, feeling their weight. "He's eternal?"

"Yes," she nodded. "And here," she motioned to another record, "are the names of those He's taken into His service. Hundreds. Thousands. Each one now lives in homes that time and decay can't touch."

Christian's throat tightened. "That's... forever."

She smiled gently. "Forever."

She read him stories next—true ones. Real accounts of people who'd walked the same path as Christian and had done unbelievable things: conquered evil kings, stood up for truth, endured fire, shut the mouths of lions. Some were scared. Some were broken. But they were all used by the Lord because they trusted Him.

"They didn't start strong," she said, as if reading Christian's thoughts. "But faith made them fierce."

Later, she led him into another room—the armory. The air smelled of steel and old wood. Along the walls hung armor: glowing helmets, shields, swords, and breastplates engraved with verses. She pointed out shoes that never wore out and a shimmering shield labeled *Faith*.

"For pilgrims like you," she said, "the Lord equips everyone who asks. He gives you what you need to fight well and finish strong."

Christian's eyes lit up as she showed him a display of legendary tools. "That's Moses' staff," she explained. "And that's the stone David used to take down Goliath. This is Jael's hammer. Gideon's trumpet. Samson's jawbone. Every one of these instruments looked ordinary—until faith touched them."

Christian was stunned. "These… were just regular people?"

"All of them. But when you walk with the Lord, even a shepherd boy can bring down a giant."

The next morning, just as he was about to leave, they stopped him again.

"One last thing," they said. "We want you to see the Delectable Mountains."

From the rooftop, they pointed south. In the distance was a breathtaking stretch of land—rolling green hills, fruit trees heavy with fruit, wildflowers swaying in the breeze, and glistening springs of water. It felt like the preview of paradise.

"What is that place?" Christian asked, wide-eyed.

"That," she said, "is *Immanuel's Land*. Every pilgrim who keeps going will get there. And when you arrive, you'll be close enough to see the gates of the Celestial City. Keep your eyes on that, no matter what happens on the road."

Christian stood in silence, tears burning in his eyes.

Hope had never looked so real.

Teen Commentary

He Gave You More Than You Think

Let's be real—sometimes, it feels like following Jesus is just one long grind. Temptations, doubts, drama, disappointments. But this scene is a reminder: God doesn't just *ask* us to follow Him—He *equips* us. He *encourages* us. And He shows us the big picture when we need it most.

At the House Beautiful, Christian gets to see how epic this journey really is. He finds out that he's part of a *legacy*—a spiritual family full of ordinary people who did extraordinary things because they trusted God. Just like *you* can.

The armory? That's not just for cool imagery. It's a picture of the real weapons you have: truth, prayer, faith, righteousness, peace. They're not flashy, but they're *unstoppable* when you actually use them.

And the view of Immanuel's Land? That's hope. A reminder that this journey ends in something *amazing*. You may not see it yet—but it's there. You're not just walking for nothing.

Reflection Questions

1. Which "weapon" or piece of spiritual armor do you feel like you use the most? Which one do you tend to forget about?

2. How does seeing the lives of past faithful people give you courage for your own challenges?

3. What would it mean for you to live like you're part of something eternal—not just surviving school or making it through the week?

4. What "Delectable Mountain" (hope or promise from God) motivates you to keep going?

Scripture Connection

"Who through faith conquered kingdoms, administered justice, and gained what was promised; who shut the mouths of lions, quenched the fury of the flames, and escaped the edge of the sword; whose weakness was turned to strength..."— *Hebrews 11:33–34 (NIV)*

Devotional Prayer

Jesus, thank You for reminding me that I'm part of something so much bigger than myself. You've given me a legacy, a purpose, and the armor I need to keep going. Help me to walk by faith like those before me, to fight with truth, and to keep my eyes on the hope ahead—Immanuel's Land. Let Your strength shine through my weakness. Amen.

LEAVING THE HILL

Christian stood at the edge of the peaceful house called *Beautiful*, the sunlight glinting off the valley below. As much as he wanted to stay in the comfort and warmth of this place, he knew it was time to keep going. The journey wasn't over—and something deep inside reminded him that comfort could never be the final destination.

Before he left, the sisters—Discretion, Piety, Charity, and Prudence—led him back into the armory.

"You can't go unprotected," Charity said. "The path ahead gets rough."

Inside, they suited him up. Not in metal, but something even stronger. Truth wrapped around his waist like a belt. Righteousness covered his chest like a custom-fit vest. He slipped on peace-laced shoes that felt like they could take him anywhere. Faith, hope, salvation, and the Word of God—each piece was carefully placed until Christian stood fully armored, ready to face whatever waited ahead.

At the gate, he paused and looked to Watchful, the porter. "Has anyone passed by recently? Another pilgrim, maybe?"

"Yes," the porter nodded. "A man named *Faithful.*"

Christian's face lit up. "Faithful! He's from my hometown—we used to live just down the street from each other. How far ahead is he?"

"Not too far," said Watchful. "He's just made it past the hill."

Christian gave him a warm handshake. "Thank you for everything. May God keep blessing you like crazy for all the kindness you've shown."

The sisters weren't ready to say goodbye just yet. "We're walking with you to the bottom," said Prudence. "That hill's not easy going down."

They talked along the way, encouraging Christian and reminding him of everything they'd taught him—truths he'd need for the dark valleys ahead. But as they reached the slope, Christian's steps slowed.

"This feels sketchy," he admitted. "Climbing up was hard, but going down? This is straight-up dangerous."

"You're not wrong," Prudence said. "This is the *Valley of Humiliation*. People slip here all the time. That's why we're going with you for this part."

Christian nodded and stepped carefully, but even with their help, he stumbled once or twice. Still, he kept going. When they reached the bottom, the sisters handed him some supplies—a loaf of bread, a small bottle of wine, and a cluster of raisins.

"You're going to need this," Piety said with a gentle smile. "Don't forget where you came from—or who walks with you."

Christian took a deep breath, gripped his staff a little tighter, and continued into the valley.

Teen Commentary

Armored Up & Headed Downhill

This scene might seem simple, but it's *packed* with truth for life—especially teen life.

Christian's just had this amazing, encouraging experience at House Beautiful (like youth camp or a spiritual high), and now it's time to go *back into real life*. And let's be honest—coming down from the high points of faith can feel even *harder* than getting there.

The Valley of Humiliation? That's like those seasons where your pride gets wrecked, your confidence takes a hit, or you just feel low and unsure of yourself. And guess what? Even though Christian's equipped and supported, he *still slips*. That's okay. What matters is that he doesn't give up—and he doesn't walk alone.

God doesn't expect you to be perfect. But He *does* give you everything you need to stand strong: truth, peace, faith, and more. And He often sends people to walk with you for part of the journey—friends, mentors, or even characters from a book like this.

So, when you're leaving your own "hilltop moment"—whether that's a retreat, a good season, or just a breakthrough—you're not going alone. You're armored up and covered in grace.

Reflection Questions

1. Have you ever come off a "spiritual high" and found it hard to keep the same energy? What helped you stay grounded?

2. Which part of God's armor do you think you need the most right now—truth, peace, faith, salvation, or God's Word?

3. What's your personal "Valley of Humiliation"? Is there a place where pride or insecurity trips you up?

4. Who's walked with you in tough times? How can you be that kind of friend for someone else?

Scripture Connection

"Put on the full armor of God, so that you can take your stand against the devil's schemes... so that when the day of evil comes, you may be able to stand your ground."— *Ephesians 6:11,13 (NIV)*

Devotional Prayer

Heavenly Father, thank You for the mountaintop moments that fill me up. But now, as I head back into the valley, remind me that You go with me. Armor me with Your truth, peace, and strength. When I stumble, lift me. When I doubt, steady me. Help me remember who I am, who You are, and that I never walk this road alone. In Jesus' name, Amen.

Scene 20

THE BATTLE WITH APOLLYON

Christian had never felt so small.

The Valley of Humiliation stretched before him, gray and quiet, except for the steady thump of his heartbeat in his ears. His boots crunched against the gravel path as fog curled around his ankles like smoke from some unseen fire.

Then—he froze.

Out of the haze lumbered a creature from nightmares. Its skin was armored in slick black scales, glinting like shattered glass. Enormous wings unfolded behind its back, cracking like thunder. Smoke and sparks poured from its nostrils, and when it spoke, its voice was a thousand growls stacked on top of each other.

"I know you," the beast snarled, stepping directly in his path. "You're one of mine."

Christian clutched the hilt of his sword, the Word, his only real weapon. His knees threatened to buckle, but he forced himself to stand tall.

"I used to be," Christian replied. "But I don't belong to you anymore. I serve the King of Zion now."

Apollyon's eyes narrowed. "You *ran* from your true king. From *me*. You broke your oath."

"I was a child when I served you," Christian said, the words shaky but true. "But I've pledged myself to a new King. His way is hard, but His love is real. I won't turn back."

The monster laughed—a cruel, burning sound. "You think He wants you? After all the times you've failed? You doubted Him in the swamp. Tried shortcuts. Slept on duty. You're a *fraud.*"

Christian flinched. Every accusation pierced like a dart. The lies... they weren't lies. But then he remembered something deeper, something stronger.

"I have failed," he said quietly. "But the King forgives. He's already healed what you broke."

That did it.

Apollyon roared and leapt, his claws lashing out. Christian raised his shield just in time. Sparks flew. The beast attacked again—dart after dart, blow after blow. One caught Christian's leg. Another slashed across his shoulder.

He cried out and staggered back, nearly dropping his sword.

Apollyon moved in, grinning with jagged teeth. "You're finished."

Christian collapsed, winded and wounded, as his sword clattered to the ground. Everything inside him screamed, *It's over.*

But then... a whisper.

A verse. A promise.

"When I fall, I will rise..."

Christian's fingers closed around the hilt of his sword. With a shout, he surged up and drove it deep into Apollyon's side.

The monster reeled back, howling. Christian pressed on, declaring, "We are more than conquerors through Him who loves us!"

Apollyon shrieked and spread his massive wings, launching himself into the air. Within seconds, he was gone—fled into the mist.

The valley was quiet again.

Christian dropped to his knees, gasping for breath. Tears streamed down his face—not of fear, but relief. A gentle hand from heaven offered him leaves of life. As he pressed them to his wounds, the pain began to fade.

He ate, drank, rested… and then stood again.

Sword still drawn.

Because the battle wasn't over—but neither was he.

Teen Commentary

Facing Your Apollyon

Ever felt like life just *hits different* some days? Like everything you ever doubted, every mistake you've made, every fear you've tried to ignore shows up in full force and stares you down?

That's Apollyon.

He's not just a fire-breathing monster—he's a symbol of every lie that tries to drag you back: *"You're not good enough." "You've messed up too many times." "God couldn't possibly love someone like you."*

But Christian stood his ground. Not because he was strong, but because he remembered Who was with him. He didn't deny his failures—he admitted them. Then, he clung to grace like his life depended on it (because it did).

You might not fight literal dragons, but you *will* face pressure, doubt, temptation, and shame. And when you do, don't run.

Pick up your sword.

Reflection Questions

1. What are some "Apollyon lies" you've believed about yourself or your relationship with God?

2. Have you ever felt like giving up in your faith because of past mistakes? What helped you hold on?

3. How can Scripture be a weapon in spiritual battles?

4. Why do you think God sometimes allows the fight rather than just removing the enemy?

Scripture Connection

"Submit yourselves therefore to God. Resist the devil, and he will flee from you." — *James 4:7*

Devotional Prayer

Heavenly Father, thank You that when the battle comes, I don't have to fight alone. Even when the enemy throws every lie and every failure in my face, remind me of the truth—that I am forgiven, chosen, and deeply loved. Strengthen my hands to hold the sword of Your Word. Help me stand when I want to fall, rise when I've been knocked down, and trust that victory is mine through You. I'm not fighting for Your love—I'm fighting from it. In Jesus' name, Amen.

Scene 21

THE VALLEY OF THE SHADOW OF DEATH

Christian stood at the edge of a narrow, cracked road that disappeared into a fog-soaked wasteland. The air was dry and cold. He'd made it through battles before, but this? This was different. The sun had vanished behind black clouds, and the silence was loud—thick with tension and fear. His hands trembled as he gripped the sword he'd fought with before.

From the edge of the valley, two guys stumbled out, pale and panicked. Dirt clung to their clothes and fear was written all over their faces.

"Where are you headed?" Christian asked, stepping cautiously toward them.

"Back," one of them said. "Anywhere but there."

"You should turn around too," the other added. "Unless you want to lose your mind… or your life."

Christian squinted into the shadows ahead. "What's in there?"

The first guy shuddered. "We didn't even go far. Barely made it back alive. We saw things—creatures, darkness that moves. We heard screams. There's no order, no light, no… hope."

Christian nodded slowly. "Even so… this is the only road to the Celestial City. I have to go."

"Suit yourself," the second guy muttered. "Just don't say we didn't warn you."

They disappeared down the path behind him. Christian turned back toward the valley. The road was barely wide enough for his feet, and on either side were deep traps—one side a bottomless ditch, the other, a bog that seemed to suck light and hope out of the air. Each step felt like walking a tightrope in the dark.

His sword glinted weakly, but the deeper he went, the more the air changed. The ground trembled. Flames flickered ahead. A cave's mouth yawned wide beside the road, spewing smoke and the stench of something unholy. Growling echoed from the pit, and strange shapes moved in the shadows. This wasn't like Apollyon. Christian's sword seemed useless here.

"God," he whispered, "please help me."

He dropped to his knees. "Lord, deliver my soul!"

A burst of flame roared out. His eyes burned. But still, he pressed forward—praying, stumbling, whispering Scripture to himself to drown out the awful voices. At one point, something whispered blasphemies into his ear—dark thoughts that chilled his soul.

"Was that... me?" he thought, shaken. "Did I really think that about God?"

Shame gripped him. He wanted to scream, run, disappear. But he couldn't stop. "No... I love Him. I didn't mean it. That wasn't me."

Just when he thought he couldn't go on, he heard something.

A voice.

Low. Calm. Confident.

"Even though I walk through the valley of the shadow of death, I will fear no evil. For You are with me."

Christian's heart skipped. Someone else was here. He wasn't alone. If someone else made it through this place... maybe he could too.

He stood up straighter. "I will walk in the strength of the Lord God!" he shouted into the darkness.

The noises backed off. Slowly. Quietly. Christian moved forward, breathing heavily, holding onto hope like a lifeline.

Then, just like that... light.

The sun rose. Warmth crept over the horizon. Christian turned and looked back, now able to see what he'd come through. Deep ditches. Shadowy figures. Gaping traps. He shivered at the thought of how close he'd come to falling.

But he hadn't.

He looked forward and saw something that looked like an old man sitting outside a cave, mumbling strange threats—but he seemed weak, stuck, powerless. Christian just walked on, a little stronger now. A little more sure.

Teen Commentary

Through the Valley

Okay, let's be real: the Valley of the Shadow of Death is *intense*. But maybe you've been there in your own way. Dark nights when God feels silent. Moments where you're wrestling with doubts, fears, or even thoughts that scare you—thoughts you're not even sure are yours.

Christian's journey through the valley reminds us of one simple truth: following Jesus isn't always sunshine and good vibes. Sometimes it's scary. Sometimes it's *silent*. But Christian didn't turn around—even when others did. He chose to pray, to walk forward, to trust... and in time, the light came.

And did you catch that powerful moment? Christian hears someone else in the valley. Just that voice reminded him he wasn't alone. You're not either.

Keep walking. Even if it's slow. Even if you're afraid. Especially then.

Reflection Questions

1. Have you ever felt like you were walking through a "valley" in your life? What helped you keep going?
2. What lies or fears have tried to whisper in your ear during your toughest moments?
3. What does it mean to "walk in the strength of the Lord" when you feel like giving up?
4. Why do you think the light came *after* Christian kept going, not before?

Scripture Connection

"Even though I walk through the valley of the shadow of death, I will fear no evil, for You are with me; Your rod and Your staff, they comfort me."—*Psalm 23:4 (NIV)*

Let this verse be your anchor. Shadows may fall, but you're never walking alone.

Devotional Prayer

Heavenly Father, when I walk through the dark valleys—the ones where fear whispers and doubt shouts—remind me that You are still with me. Even when I can't see You, help me trust that You haven't left. When shame or lies try to pull me down, speak truth louder in my heart. Give me strength to keep walking, one step at a time, knowing that the light will come. And until it does, help me hold tight to You. In Jesus' name, Amen.

Scene 22

CHRISTIAN MEETS FAITHFUL

Christian stood on a small hill, the sun warming his back as he looked ahead down the road. Off in the distance, a familiar figure trudged forward, backpack bouncing with every step.

"Hey! Wait up!" Christian called, waving both arms like a man stranded on an island. "It's me! Christian!"

The other teen glanced back. It was Faithful—his old neighbor from the city they'd both fled. Faithful didn't stop. "Can't! I'm running for my life. There's danger behind me!"

That got Christian's heart racing. He pushed forward, legs pumping harder until he caught up and even passed his friend, puffing with pride.

But just as he turned to flash a grin, his foot caught a rock. He went flying, face-first into the dust. Wind knocked out, he groaned, struggling to get up. Faithful reached him, helped him to his feet without a word of judgment.

They walked side-by-side now, pace slower but hearts lighter.

"Man, I'm glad I caught up to you," Christian said. "It's better doing this journey with someone."

Faithful nodded. "I always hoped we'd travel together. But after you left, I had to make the choice alone. People in the city wouldn't stop talking about you—said fire from heaven was going to destroy everything."

Christian's eyes widened. "Wait—seriously? Did anyone else leave?"

"Nope. Lots of talk, no action. Some mocked you. Called you crazy. I believed it, though. I couldn't stay. I had to get out."

"Did you hear anything about Pliable?" Christian asked.

Faithful gave a dry chuckle. "He tried following you—but bailed at the first sign of trouble. Now he pretends it never happened. People laugh at him. Won't even give him a job. He's worse off than before."

Christian sighed. "I had hopes for him. But turning back like that... it's like a dog going back to its own vomit."

Faithful gave a sad nod. "Yeah... sometimes people mock what they don't understand. He became a warning."

As they walked, Christian asked about the road so far.

"Oh, I dodged the swamp you fell in," Faithful said. "But I ran into this girl—WANTON. She was all smiles and flirty whispers. Promised all kinds of pleasure. It was hard to say no."

Christian's brow furrowed. "That's the same temptation Joseph faced. But he ran. Did you?"

"I didn't give in, but I struggled. It was close. I remembered this old verse—something about her steps leading to hell. I shut my eyes and walked away."

"Close calls are still victories," Christian said. "Thank God you resisted."

Faithful continued sharing stories—an old man named Adam the First tried to recruit him with promises of luxury and pleasure. But when Faithful noticed a message on the man's forehead—"Put off the old man with his deeds"—he refused. Still, Adam's grip left him bruised and shaken.

"Moses showed up after that," Faithful said. "Strict, scary guy. Knocked me flat. Said I deserved it. I begged for mercy, but he didn't know how to show it. I would've died if someone hadn't stopped him."

"Who?" Christian asked.

"I didn't know him at first. But then I saw the scars on his hands and side. It was Him. The Lord."

Christian nodded. "Moses brings the Law, but he can't save. Only Jesus can."

Faithful described more trials: the Valley of Humility, Discontent trying to pull him back, Shame mocking his faith.

"He told me being religious was pathetic," Faithful said. "That I'd lose respect, friends, fun. He made me feel small. I almost gave in."

"But you didn't."

"Nope. I realized: Shame can't speak for God. The world laughs now, but God's the real judge. So I told Shame to get lost."

The two friends walked on, the road dusty but lighter with the comfort of shared battle scars and unwavering faith.

Teen Commentary

Real Friends, Real Fights, Real Faith

Let's be real—Faithful's journey sounds like a highlight reel of *everything* teens struggle with. Temptation? Check. Peer pressure? Double check. Identity crisis? Absolutely. And yet, what makes this scene powerful is not just the drama, but how honest and *relatable* it is.

We all want companions on our faith journey. People who get it. Who've fallen too, but get back up. Christian and Faithful show us that having someone walk with you makes a huge difference—and that pride, shame, and temptation are things everyone wrestles with, even the "strong" believers.

Did you notice how Faithful handled Shame? He didn't argue with him using memes or sarcasm—he remembered *who God is*. He trusted that what *God says is best* really *is* best, even if the world rolls its eyes.

That's courage. Not flashy, superhero courage—but the kind of strength it takes to say, "I don't care if I'm the only one. I'm still going with Jesus."

And hey, sometimes we *do* trip up like Christian did. But that's when we need friends who'll help us back up—not brag that they're ahead.

Reflection Questions

1. Who are the "Faithful" people in your life—those who encourage your walk with God? How can you be that kind of friend to someone else?
2. When have you felt the pressure of "Shame" trying to make you embarrassed about your faith? How did you respond—or how *could* you respond differently next time?
3. What does "temptation" look like in your world right now? How can remembering Scripture (like Faithful did) help you stay strong?
4. Have you ever tried to go it alone on your spiritual journey? What happened—and what might be different if you had a companion?

Scripture Connection

"I am not ashamed of the gospel, because it is the power of God that brings salvation to everyone who believes…" —*Romans 1:16 (NIV)*

Let that verse be your anthem when Shame comes knocking. You're not weak for following Jesus—you're strong enough to swim upstream.

Devotional Prayer

Heavenly Father, thank You for friends who walk the road of faith with me. Thank You for the ones who pick me up when I fall, who point me back to You when I drift. Help me be that kind of friend too—honest, humble, and full of grace. When temptation calls and shame tries to silence me, give me courage to stand firm. Let my faith be real, not perfect—but real. And remind me that I don't have to walk this road alone. In Jesus' name, Amen.

Scene 23

TALKATIVE

The sun was starting to drop behind the hills, casting long shadows over the dusty path. Faithful glanced to his right and noticed a tall guy walking a few feet off the trail. The guy looked impressive—confident stride, well-dressed, good posture. From a distance, he seemed cool.

"Hey there," Faithful called out. "You headed the same way we are—toward the Celestial City?"

The guy turned with a smooth smile. "That's exactly where I'm going."

Faithful smiled, relieved. "Awesome. Then maybe we can walk together?"

"With pleasure," the guy said, moving closer. "Name's Talkative."

Faithful nodded. "Nice to meet you. I'm Faithful. This is Christian, my friend."

Talkative extended a hand but didn't really wait for a response before diving into his favorite topic—talking.

"I love deep conversations," Talkative said, already sounding like a podcast host. "Most people waste time gossiping or talking nonsense. But I enjoy the real stuff—faith, eternity, purpose."

Christian hung back a little, letting Faithful take the lead.

Faithful's eyes lit up. "Me too. What better use of words than to talk about the things of God?"

"Exactly!" Talkative said. "Miracles, mysteries, doctrine—I could go on for hours. Scripture is full of fascinating truths. Talking about repentance, salvation, and the new birth? It doesn't get better than that."

Faithful nodded thoughtfully. "It's true. But we should talk to grow in truth, not just to fill the air. Right?"

"Of course," Talkative replied easily. "That's what I said. It's about learning and sharing the Gospel—debating, discussing, teaching. I've got loads of Scripture on all of it."

Faithful gave a small nod but slowed down, letting Christian catch up. "Hey," he said quietly, "this guy seems solid, doesn't he? He knows his stuff."

Christian gave a small, knowing smile. "He *sounds* solid. But trust me—he's not who you think he is."

Faithful blinked. "You know him?"

"Know him?" Christian laughed softly. "Too well. He's from my hometown—Prating Row. He's all talk, no walk. The kind of guy who quotes Bible verses at church, but is a nightmare at home. Loud about Jesus on Sunday, cruel and careless on Monday."

Faithful looked surprised. "But he seems so sincere."

"Yeah, from far away. Like a painting that looks beautiful from across the room, but when you get close, it's all messy brushstrokes."

Faithful frowned. "So what do we do?"

Christian looked ahead. "You really want to know what's in his heart? Ask him a real question. Something personal. He loves theory, but he dodges truth."

So Faithful did.

As they walked on, he turned to Talkative again. "Alright, Talkative—here's one for you. How does God's saving grace actually show itself in someone's life?"

Talkative perked up. "Great question! Well, it makes people really mad at sin. That's the first sign."

Faithful raised an eyebrow. "Are you sure? I mean, someone can shout about sin but still secretly love it. Isn't hating sin something deeper—something that changes how we live?"

Talkative hesitated, clearly caught off guard.

Faithful continued, "Look, anyone can *say* they hate sin. But real grace changes your heart and your habits. It makes you want Jesus, not just want to win an argument. Don't you think?"

Talkative chuckled nervously. "You're digging a little deep, aren't you? I mean, why so personal?"

Faithful didn't back off. "Because this is about *truth*. Not just talk. Do *you* live this stuff? Or do you just like to sound smart?"

Talkative's face flushed, and he stiffened. "I don't see why I have to prove myself to you. I came here for a chat, not an interrogation."

Faithful looked him in the eye. "Then maybe this journey's not for you."

Talkative muttered something under his breath and gradually drifted off the path, pretending he had somewhere else to be.

Christian joined Faithful. "Well done," he said quietly. "Now you've seen it for yourself."

Faithful shook his head, disappointed. "He had all the right words…"

Christian nodded. "But not the right heart. That's the difference between *knowing* truth and *living* it."

Teen Commentary

Talk Is Cheap

Let's be real: we've all met a *Talkative*. Someone who knows all the Bible answers, who shows up for youth group, who sounds spiritual—but when you actually get close, the fruit just isn't there. It's all style, no substance.

Faithful was impressed at first. Talkative had Christian lingo down. But Christian saw through the hype. Why? Because *true faith shows up in the details*—how you treat your family, how you act when no one's watching, what you prioritize when life gets tough.

It's easy to say you follow Jesus. But following means footsteps, not just phrases.

Jesus doesn't just want your words. He wants your *heart*. And that heart change will always show up in how you live.

Reflection Questions

1. When do you find it easiest to talk like a Christian but hardest to live like one?

2. Have you ever been "Talkative" without realizing it? What woke you up?

3. How can you tell the difference between someone who *knows* truth and someone who *lives* it?

4. What's one area of your life where you want your faith to be more than just words?

Scripture Connection

"Do not merely listen to the word, and so deceive yourselves. Do what it says."— *James 1:22 (NIV)*

Devotional Prayer

God, sometimes I get caught up in sounding good instead of living well. Help me not to be all talk and no action. Give me a heart that matches my words—a heart that loves You deeply and shows it in how I live, not just what I say. When I'm tempted to impress others or hide behind phrases, remind me that You see what's really inside. Help me walk honestly with You, with courage to live out my faith every day. In Jesus' name, Amen.

Scene 24

EVANGELIST'S WARNING

The woods began to thin, and the light ahead hinted at open ground. Christian and Faithful pushed on, dusty and tired but more determined than ever.

Faithful glanced over his shoulder. "Wait... someone's coming."

Christian turned, squinting into the sunlight. Then a smile broke across his face. "It's Evangelist!"

Faithful grinned. "That guy saved my life. He showed me the gate. I owe him everything."

Evangelist strode up the path, his eyes warm and steady, like someone who knew where he was going—and why.

"Peace be with you, my dear friends," he said, his voice strong but gentle. "And to those who walk beside you."

Christian stepped forward and hugged him. "You have no idea how much it means to see you again. Just the sight of your face reminds me of why I started this journey."

Faithful nodded. "You're always welcome. Your words lit our way when we didn't even know we were walking in the dark."

Evangelist placed a hand on each of their shoulders. "Tell me everything. What's happened since we last spoke? What trials have you faced? How have you stayed on the path?"

The two of them took turns, talking about Vanity Fair, the Hill of Difficulty, the valleys, the traps, the victories. Evangelist listened without interrupting, nodding now and then, his expression proud yet serious.

"I'm glad," Evangelist said finally. "Not glad that the road's been hard—but glad that you've endured. You've kept walking, even when the ground shook and the night felt endless. That matters. It really does."

He took a deep breath. "But don't get too comfortable. The hardest part might still be ahead."

Christian's face fell slightly. "There's more?"

Evangelist nodded. "You're almost out of the wilderness. But soon you'll reach a city. From the outside, it looks like a regular place. People, streets, noise. But inside—it's a war zone. And they're not just going to make fun of you. They'll hate you. One of you, maybe both, will pay for your faith with your life."

Faithful swallowed hard, glancing at Christian. "Wait. One of us will die?"

Evangelist's eyes met theirs. "Yes. But hear me clearly—death for truth is not defeat. It's a crown. It's glory. The one who dies will enter the Celestial City first. The other will suffer longer but will still win. Neither of you loses—unless you quit."

Christian stood a little taller. "If that's what it takes, so be it."

Evangelist stepped closer, his voice dropping low. "You're not out of enemy territory yet. Satan is still hunting. He's smart. He's subtle.

So guard your hearts. Don't get attached to anything here. The world will try to pull you in with comfort, compromise, and noise. Don't let it. Keep your eyes locked on the Kingdom—even when you can't see it."

Faithful nodded slowly. "It's hard to imagine that kind of pressure."

"It is," Evangelist said. "But you won't face it alone. Heaven is with you. You've been given power. Use it. Stand like warriors. And when the moment comes, trust your King to carry your soul."

Christian exhaled. "Thank you. Truly."

Evangelist stepped back. "I may not see you again in this life. But I'll be watching for you at the gates."

And with that, he turned and disappeared into the trees.

Teen Commentary

Hold Fast. The Real Fight Is Coming.

This is one of the most intense moments in *The Pilgrim's Progress*. Evangelist doesn't sugarcoat anything. He shows up, hugs his guys, and tells them the truth: Faith isn't safe. Following Jesus isn't a chill hike through the woods—it's a *battle*. And sometimes, there's a price.

But here's the twist: death isn't the loss. Quitting is. The one who dies for Jesus? He wins faster. The one who suffers longer? Still wins. Why? Because both keep their eyes locked on the Kingdom.

Evangelist is like the coach before the final round. He doesn't tell Christian and Faithful to avoid pain—he tells them to *fight through it*. And he reminds them: they're not alone. Heaven is on their side.

This scene is raw and real. It's not just a pep talk—it's a warning and a call to courage. And it's meant for us too.

Reflection Questions

1. What's one comfort in your life that could distract you from following Jesus with everything?

2. Has your faith ever cost you something—like a friendship, popularity, or an opportunity?

3. What does it look like for you to "set your face like flint" (be unshakable) in your daily life?

4. How can you remind yourself that "Heaven is on your side" when things get hard?

Scripture Connection

"Let us not become weary in doing good, for at the proper time we will reap a harvest if we do not give up."— *Galatians 6:9 (NIV)*

Devotional Prayer

Heavenly Father, sometimes following You feels like a battle—and that's hard to face. When the road gets rough and the pressure builds, help me stand firm and not give up. Remind me that even if I suffer or lose things for Your name's sake, You are with me and the victory is sure. Give me courage to keep my eyes on You, to hold fast when everything tries to pull me away. Thank You for being my strength and my reward—help me trust You completely, no matter what comes. In Jesus' name, Amen.

Scene 25

VANITY FAIR

The gravel path that Christian and Faithful had been walking on finally gave way to paved streets, buzzing with music, bright lights, and flashy billboards. Ahead of them rose a city of color and chaos, a place pulsing with life and noise.

"Whoa," Faithful said, shielding his eyes. "What is this place?"

"Looks like a never-ending street party," Christian muttered. His stomach turned—not with fear, but with unease. This wasn't just a town. This was *Vanity Fair*.

The fair sprawled for blocks. Food trucks, pop-up shops, carnival games, influencers livestreaming, and performers on every corner. You could buy anything here—fame, followers, cash, designer clothes, even fake happiness wrapped in glitter and sold with a discount code. Everyone smiled, laughed, and posed for the camera. It looked perfect.

But something felt...off.

As soon as Christian and Faithful stepped into the fair, the crowd slowed. Whispers passed between painted lips. Phones angled toward them.

"Who *are* they?" a guy in ripped jeans asked.

"Is this a cosplay thing?" a girl giggled, eyeing their plain, travel-worn clothes. "They look like they walked out of a medieval Bible camp."

Christian kept his head down, heart racing. Faithful stood tall beside him.

A street vendor shoved a flashy watch in their face. "You boys wanna live a little? This will make you *somebody*."

Faithful shook his head. "No thanks. We're just passing through."

Another vendor leaned over his booth, eyes sharp. "What *do* you want then?"

Christian looked him straight in the eye. "We're here for truth."

Everything stopped.

People stared, mouths open. Then the laughter came—loud and mocking.

"You serious?" someone scoffed. "Truth? What even is that anymore?"

"Look at these freaks," a voice shouted. "Too good for the rest of us!"

Suddenly, Christian and Faithful were surrounded. The crowd pressed in, jeering, some throwing slushies or snapping pics. "Go back to whatever cult you came from!"

They didn't fight. They didn't insult back. They just stood their ground, eyes lifted like they saw something no one else could.

"Arrest them!" someone cried. "They're starting trouble!"

Rough hands grabbed them. They were dragged through the crowd, beaten, smeared with garbage, and locked in a cage at the center of the fair. A sign was slapped on the front: *Dangerous Lunatics — Stay Away.*

Still, they didn't shout. They prayed.

Some people kept laughing. But others... started watching.

"Wait," a teen girl whispered to her friend. "They're not yelling. They're not even mad."

"I think they're... peaceful?" her friend replied, confused. "Like they actually believe in what they're saying."

Others began to question, but as soon as they did, they were mocked too. Tension grew until fights broke out among the crowd. The authorities blamed the pilgrims and dragged them out again—this time chained, bloodied, but still calm.

When they were returned to their cage, Faithful leaned close and whispered, "Evangelist told us this might happen. He said suffering might come—but the reward is worth it."

Christian nodded. "Whatever happens, we trust God. Even if one of us dies... the victory's already won."

They looked through the bars—not with hate, not with fear—but with hope.

Teen Commentary

Why Vanity Fair Feels So Familiar

Let's be real: *Vanity Fair* isn't just some old-fashioned village in a dusty book. It's *your* social media feed, the mall, your school, or that party you felt weird at because you didn't want to compromise your values.

Christian and Faithful walked into a world where they didn't fit. They didn't speak the same language (literally and spiritually), they didn't dress the same, and most importantly—they didn't *want* what the world was selling. They wanted **truth**.

The moment they said that out loud, the world turned on them.

Sound familiar?

Living as a Christian today means walking through *Vanity Fair* all the time. You'll be tempted with popularity, comfort, money, relationships, and shortcuts to "success." But choosing to follow Jesus may make you stand out—and not in a glamorous way.

But here's the kicker: *you're not alone.* And you're not crazy for saying "no" to the world and "yes" to something greater. In fact, that kind of courage speaks louder than any viral trend. Some will laugh. Some will get mad. But others? They'll start to notice—and wonder.

Christian and Faithful's quiet faith under pressure wasn't weakness. It was *strength.* And it pointed others to a Kingdom bigger than the fair.

Reflection Questions

1. What are some "vanities" you see being sold in today's culture that try to distract you from your walk with God?
2. Have you ever felt like an outsider because of your faith? How did you respond?
3. What does it mean to "buy the truth" in your daily life? How do you live it out?
4. How can you show love and patience to those who mock or misunderstand your faith?

Scripture Connection

"Do not conform to the pattern of this world, but be transformed by the renewing of your mind. Then you will be able to test and approve what God's will is—his good, pleasing and perfect will." — *Romans 12:2 (NIV)*

Devotional Prayer

Heavenly Father, walking through a world full of noise, temptation, and pressure can feel overwhelming. When everyone around me chases after things that don't last, help me stand firm in the truth of who You are. Give me courage to say no to the distractions and yes to You—even when it means feeling out of place or being misunderstood. Remind me that my identity is found in You, not in what the world offers. Help me reflect Your peace and love, even when I face rejection or ridicule. Thank You for being my strength and my hope. In Jesus' name, Amen.

Scene 26

THE TRIAL OF FAITHFUL

The town square buzzed with tension. Faithful stood alone in the center, chains on his wrists, bruises blooming beneath his shirt. The crowd had packed in tight—some out of curiosity, some with clenched fists and cruel smirks. At the head of the court, robed in dark red with a crooked grin stretched across his face, sat Judge Hategood.

"This court is now in session!" barked the bailiff. "The case of the people of Vanity versus Faithful the Pilgrim!"

Faithful raised his head. His eyes, clear and steady, scanned the room without fear.

"You're accused of disturbing the peace," the judge sneered, "corrupting the people with dangerous ideas, and slandering our glorious prince Beelzebub. How do you plead?"

Faithful's voice was calm, almost gentle. "I only spoke the truth—truth that opposes lies which have enslaved too many for too long. I've harmed no one. I come in peace. But yes—I stand against Beelzebub. He's the enemy of my King, and I owe him no allegiance."

Gasps rippled through the room.

"Order!" yelled Judge Hategood, slamming his gavel. "Let the witnesses speak!"

From the crowd emerged three smug figures—Envy, Superstition, and Pickthank.

Envy swaggered forward first, his eyes full of malice. "My lord, this man's dangerous. He teaches that faith and holiness matter more than our traditions. He claims that our town's way of life is wicked."

The judge nodded. "Horrifying. Go on."

Superstition stepped up, arms crossed. "He told me my religion was pointless—that without divine truth, we're all just pretending. That we're doomed if we keep this up."

Judge Hategood raised an eyebrow. "The nerve."

Then came Pickthank. He rolled his eyes like a drama queen. "He insults our prince, trashes our noble leaders—Lord Oldman, Sir Having Greedy, and my dear friend, Mr. Lechery. He even called you, my lord, an 'ungodly villain.'"

The judge looked mildly offended, though mostly amused. "Charming. And what say you, Faithful?"

Faithful stood tall. "Everything I've said aligns with what God has revealed. If you can prove me wrong, I'll admit it here and now. But your leaders, your prince, this entire system—you're all on the wrong side of truth. You worship comfort, pleasure, and pride. I follow the One who calls people out of darkness."

The room erupted. Shouts. Laughter. Anger. The jury—twelve men with names like Mr. Blind-Man, Mr. No-Good, and Mr. Cruelty—didn't need long.

"Guilty," they all said.

"Sentence?" asked the judge, barely containing his glee.

"Death," said Mr. Hate-Light. "The crueler, the better."

And so, they dragged Faithful out. They whipped him, mocked him, stabbed him, stoned him, and finally burned him. The crowd cheered as flames rose, unaware of what happened next.

From behind the smoke, a golden chariot descended from the sky. As Faithful's body fell, his soul was lifted—bright, whole, and free. Trumpets sounded. Heaven opened. And he was gone—finally home.

Back in the prison, Christian wept—but not from sorrow alone. Hope had begun to stir in the crowd. One young man—Hopeful—watched everything and whispered to himself, "I want what he had."

Hopeful would soon rise from Faithful's ashes.

Teen Commentary

Standing for Faith When It's Not Popular

Let's be real—this scene hits *hard*. Faithful wasn't out there being a jerk or picking fights. He just lived what he believed, and the world around him *couldn't handle it*. Sound familiar? Maybe not with fire and whips, but you've probably felt pressure to shut up about your faith, act like it doesn't matter, or blend in when everything inside you says *this isn't right*.

What makes this scene powerful is that Faithful doesn't lash out, beg for mercy, or cave under pressure. He's calm. Confident. Clear. Not because he's fearless, but because he knows where his hope is.

And the ending? Wow. While the world thinks they've won, God's like, *"Actually, he just leveled up."* Faithful's death isn't the end—it's his entrance into something eternal. His stand plants a seed in Hopeful, and probably others watching too.

Truth: Living boldly for Jesus might not make you popular, but it will leave a mark—and maybe even change someone else's life.

Reflection Questions

1. Have you ever felt pressured to hide or water down your faith? What did you do?

2. What does it mean to "speak truth in love"? How do you live that out in a world that may not want to hear it?

3. Who is someone in your life that's been a "Faithful" for you—someone who lived boldly for Jesus and inspired you?

4. If you were on trial for being a Christian, would there be enough evidence to convict you?

Scripture Connection

"Indeed, all who desire to live a godly life in Christ Jesus will be persecuted."—*2 Timothy 3:12 (ESV)*

Devotional Prayer

Heavenly Father, standing firm when the world pushes back isn't easy. Sometimes following You means facing rejection, pain, or even loneliness. Help me, like Faithful, to speak Your truth calmly and clearly—even when it's unpopular or costly. Give me strength to trust that You see every struggle and every step I take for You. When I feel afraid or tempted to stay silent, remind me that You are my hope and my reward. Thank You for the promise of eternal life and for using my faith to inspire others, just like Faithful's courage sparked hope in Hopeful. In Jesus' name, Amen.

Scene 27

THE CURIOUS CASE OF MR. BY-ENDS

The sun had just started slipping behind the trees as Christian and Hopeful walked out of the noisy market town. They were tired, but relieved. That fair had been chaotic—temptation dressed in glitter and gold—and they were more than ready for peace again.

Up ahead, they saw someone strolling along the path, hands in his pockets, whistling like he didn't have a care in the world.

"Hey there!" Christian called out. "Mind if we walk with you?"

The man turned, giving them a friendly grin. "Not at all. I'm heading to the Celestial City too."

"Cool," Hopeful said. "Where are you from?"

"Fairspeech," the man replied smoothly. "Nice place, good people, good business."

Christian raised an eyebrow. "Fairspeech, huh? Ever heard the saying, 'Don't trust someone just because they talk nice'?"

The man laughed. "That's harsh. I hope I'm not one of those people."

Christian asked his name, but the man danced around the question. "Names don't matter much when we're all going the same way. But if you must know, some people call me Mr. By-Ends. It's not my real name, just something haters say."

Christian gave Hopeful a glance. "I think we've heard of you."

Mr. By-Ends didn't seem phased. He went on to talk about how well-connected he was—related to Lord Turn-About, Mr. Facing-Both-Ways, even the fancy-sounding Mr. Two-Tongues. He explained how his family had a long tradition of going whichever way the wind blew. "It's a talent, really," he said proudly. "Why fight the current when you can float with it and still end up in the right place?"

Hopeful blinked. "So you follow God... when it's popular?"

"Well, yeah," Mr. By-Ends shrugged. "Isn't that when it makes the most sense? I mean, we're not supposed to make life harder than it needs to be, right? Why struggle?"

Christian frowned. "Following Christ means walking with Him when He's in chains and when He's celebrated. If you're only in it for the applause, you're not following Him—you're following yourself."

Mr. By-Ends smiled, unaffected. "Suit yourself. I'll catch up with some folks who think more like me."

As they walked on, Christian and Hopeful saw three men catching up to Mr. By-Ends. He welcomed them like old friends. Their names? Mr. Hold-the-World, Mr. Money-Love, and Mr. Save-All. They had gone to the same school, taught by Mr. Gripeman, a master of selfish gain.

Their conversation turned toward faith—as a means to get ahead in life.

Mr. Money-Love asked, "Is it really wrong if someone uses religion to make life better? Like a preacher who changes his style to get a bigger church? Or a shopkeeper who gets more customers by acting more spiritual?"

Mr. By-Ends beamed. "Exactly my point!"

When they finally caught up to Christian and Hopeful, they challenged them with that same question.

Christian didn't flinch. "Even a baby Christian knows the answer to that. You don't follow Jesus for what He gives you—you follow Him because He is the Way. Jesus saw crowds follow Him just for bread, but He called them out. We don't come to God for perks; we come for life."

And with that, Christian and Hopeful walked on, leaving the crowd-pleasers behind.

Teen Commentary

Real or Just Convenient?

Let's be honest—sometimes it's tempting to follow Jesus only when it's easy. When your friends go to youth group, when posting a Bible verse gets you likes, when standing up for your faith costs nothing. Mr. By-Ends was all about *comfortable Christianity*—faith that worked for his reputation, success, or whatever was trending. He liked the *idea* of the Celestial City, but not if it meant giving up popularity or profit.

Sound familiar?

In a world where everyone's about clout, image, and hustle, it's easy to make faith just another thing that helps you "get ahead." But Christian reminds us: if you're only with Jesus when He's "popular," you're not really with Him. Real faith is faithful even when it's inconvenient, uncomfortable, or unpopular.

Jesus doesn't want fans. He wants followers.

Reflection Questions

1. Have you ever been tempted to follow Jesus just because it was convenient or cool?

2. In what ways do people today treat religion like a business opportunity or social strategy?

3. What does it *really* mean to follow Jesus "against wind and tide"?

4. If your faith suddenly cost you something—friends, comfort, reputation—would you still follow?

Scripture Connection

"Jesus answered, 'Very truly I tell you, you are looking for me, not because you saw the signs I performed but because you ate the loaves and had your fill.'" —*John 6:26*

This verse reminds us that Jesus sees our *true* motives—and He invites us to something deeper than just chasing blessings. He calls us to chase Him.

Devotional Prayer

Heavenly Father, help me not to follow You only when it's easy or popular. Give me courage to stand firm, even when it's uncomfortable or costs me something. Teach me to follow Jesus for who He truly is—not for what I can get. Keep my heart faithful, no matter what the world says. In Jesus' name, Amen.

DEMAS: THE TRAP AT SILVER RIDGE

The trail had finally leveled out. After miles of rough hills and stressful detours, Christian and Hopeful were more than happy to walk in peace. The sun cast a soft glow over a quiet stretch of grassy land known as "Ease." It was the kind of place where you could breathe again.

"I could stay here forever," Hopeful said, stretching his arms wide.

Christian nodded. "Yeah... but it won't last long. This path is narrow, and we'll be through it before we know it."

And sure enough, just as the scenery began to shift, they saw a strange hill jutting out in the distance. It sparkled oddly under the sun, like something half-buried was trying to break free.

On one side of the hill, a man stood waving at them, dressed sharply, like he'd stepped out of some high-end fashion ad. He had a polished smile and a confident tone.

"Hey, you two!" he called. "Come check this out—it's worth your time!"

Hopeful slowed. "What's he pointing at?"

The man grinned. "Just over here—there's a silver mine. Real treasure, not the fake stuff. People are digging right now. You could cash in with just a little work. No tricks."

Hopeful's eyes lit up. "Treasure? You think it's legit?"

Christian shook his head sharply. "Nope. I've heard of this place. It's dangerous. People get obsessed, wander too close, and the ground gives way. Some fall in and never come back. Others are hurt so bad they never recover."

Christian called out, "Isn't this mine a trap for travelers? Haven't people died chasing what's down there?"

The man, who introduced himself as *Demas*, chuckled. "Only those who were careless. If you're smart, you'll be fine." But even as he spoke, he looked away, a blush creeping up his neck.

Hopeful glanced back at Christian, unsure. "Maybe it's worth just taking a look?"

Christian stepped in front of him. "Hopeful, don't. This kind of shortcut never leads anywhere good. We're not here to get rich. We're here to get home."

"Suit yourselves," Demas said, still smiling. "But if you change your minds, I'll be right here."

As they walked past, Christian leaned over and whispered, "Watch— when By-Ends shows up, I bet he'll head straight to the mine."

Hopeful nodded. "No doubt. Guys like him can't resist that kind of thing."

Demas called out again, more insistent this time. "Come on! What are you afraid of? I'm one of you. I'm a believer, too!"

Christian stopped and turned, firm. "You're no friend of the path. You've already been judged for turning away from the King's road, and now you want to pull others down with you. I know your type—your family tree is full of men who traded truth for treasure. Gehazi, Judas… and now you."

Demas shifted uncomfortably but said nothing more.

Christian turned to Hopeful. "Let's keep going. We'll report this when we get to the King."

As they walked on, Christian looked back just in time to see By-Ends and his crew arrive and veer off toward Demas without hesitation.

"Guess they made their choice," Hopeful said quietly.

"They won't be seen again," Christian replied.

They kept moving forward, the road narrow but safe, their hearts a little heavier—but their steps more certain.

Teen Commentary

Let's be real: there's always going to be a *Demas* calling you off the path. It might be money, popularity, image, or that "easy win" that promises a shortcut to happiness. It's not always obviously wrong—it's *shiny*. That's the point. It's appealing, and the danger is hidden just under the surface.

Christian saw right through it. He knew what mattered most wasn't a quick reward—it was finishing the journey *with integrity*. The world may offer a million things that look good, but if they pull you away from God's path, they're not blessings—they're bait.

Demas wasn't just a random guy. He claimed to be "one of them," which is exactly what makes temptations like his so sneaky. He looked successful, confident, and even spiritual. But his heart was hooked on the world.

Christian didn't fall for it. Will you?

Reflection Questions

1. What are some "silver mines" in your life—things that promise happiness but might pull you off course?

2. Why do you think temptations often come from people who seem trustworthy or "religious"?

3. How can you tell the difference between a *blessing* from God and a *distraction* from the enemy?

4. What helps you stay focused on your walk with God when the world offers easier options?

Scripture Connection

"For Demas, because he loved this world, has deserted me and has gone to Thessalonica."—*2 Timothy 4:10*

This verse reminds us that even close companions can drift when the love of the world takes over. Stay alert. Stay faithful. Keep walking.

Devotional Prayer

Heavenly Father, help me see through the shiny traps that promise easy rewards but pull me away from You. Give me strength to stay on Your narrow path, even when shortcuts look tempting. Keep my heart fixed on You, not on the world's distractions. In Jesus' name, Amen.

Scene 29

REMEMBER LOT'S WIFE

The path leveled out as Christian and Hopeful crossed into a quiet stretch of dry, sunbaked land. The heat shimmered in the distance, and the silence pressed around them like a heavy blanket. They didn't talk much—each lost in thought after escaping the temptations of Lucre Hill.

That's when they saw it.

Just off the road stood a strange monument. At first glance, it looked like a weathered statue. But the longer they stared, the more unsettling it became. It wasn't just a statue. It looked like… a person. A woman, frozen in mid-turn, face twisted—not in fear, but in regret. Her whole form was stiff, like she'd been stopped in time. Salt crusted her features like ash from a long-dead fire.

Hopeful squinted. "Dude… what is *that*?"

Christian stepped closer. "It's not just a statue." He pointed to an inscription carved at the top. The letters were oddly shaped, some nearly worn away, but readable. "'Remember Lot's Wife,'" he read aloud.

Hopeful's face paled. "No way. *That's* her? From the Bible? She looked back… and *this* is what happened to her?"

Christian nodded solemnly. "Yeah. She was escaping Sodom—running toward safety. But her heart was still stuck back there. She looked back with longing… and paid the price."

Hopeful looked shaken. "Man… if we had listened to Demas and wandered toward Lucre Hill, we might've ended up like her. Honestly, I almost went." He kicked at a pebble on the path. "What was I even thinking? Her sin was just looking back. I *wanted* to go. That could've been *me*."

Christian put a hand on his shoulder. "It's God's grace that you didn't. We've gotta remember this. She escaped one judgment—she got out of Sodom—but still ended up destroyed because she couldn't let go. She became a warning sign for people like us."

Hopeful nodded slowly. "She's like a living caution tape."

Christian's eyes drifted toward the hill in the distance. "And Demas is still there, digging for treasure in a place cursed by greed. It's like robbing someone while standing in front of a judge. Or stealing wallets at the base of a gallows."

Hopeful gave a dry laugh. "How blind do you have to be to ignore a statue like that right in front of you?"

"Pretty blind," Christian said. "Or maybe desperate. Maybe they just want what they want so badly, they can't even see how close they are to disaster."

They stood in silence for a moment, the wind whispering around the salt-crusted figure.

"I should've been that statue," Hopeful whispered.

"But you're not," Christian replied. "And that's a reason to be thankful. Let's remember what we've seen here. Let's not just run from judgment, but *run with our hearts fully turned forward.* No looking back."

Hopeful nodded. "No looking back."

Teen Commentary

What's the Big Deal About Looking Back?

Okay, so this part might seem a little dramatic. A woman turns into salt just for *looking back*? But here's the deeper issue: Lot's wife didn't just glance over her shoulder. Her *heart* was still attached to the world God told her to leave behind. That longing? That hesitation? It showed where her real treasure was.

This moment in *The Pilgrim's Progress* is a wake-up call. It's not just about avoiding bad stuff—it's about fully committing to what's ahead. Christian and Hopeful had just walked away from a get-rich-quick temptation. They were *this close* to chasing shiny things that looked good on the outside but were soul-killers on the inside.

Lot's wife? She reminds us what happens when we try to move forward with God while clinging to our old life. That salt statue wasn't just a judgment—it was a *signpost* for all of us.

Reflection Questions

1. What's something from your past or your "old life" that you still feel tempted to look back at?

2. How can you tell if your heart is truly focused on where God is leading you?

3. Why do you think people are willing to risk everything for "treasures" that don't last?

4. Can you think of a time when God's mercy helped you avoid a mistake or a trap—just in time?

Scripture Connection

"Remember Lot's wife." —*Luke 17:32 (ESV)*

Jesus himself drops this one-liner as a serious warning. Short. Sharp. And unforgettable. He's basically saying: Don't half-follow me. Don't drag your past sins into your future. Don't look back. You're not called to be a salt statue. You're called to move forward.

Devotional Prayer

Heavenly Father, help me keep my eyes and heart focused on You—not on the past or things You've called me to leave behind. When the world tries to pull me back, give me the strength to move forward with faith and courage. Thank You for Your mercy that keeps me from stumbling. In Jesus' name, Amen.

Scene 30

RESPITE BY THE RIVER

Christian flopped down on the soft grass, letting out a long, relieved sigh. "Finally," he muttered, arms behind his head as he stared up at a sky so blue it looked like it had been painted just for them.

Hopeful dropped his pack beside him and laughed. "I'm not even tired anymore. This place is unreal."

And it really was.

They had wandered into a place that felt like a dream—like the kind of peaceful scene you only saw in those perfect Instagram travel reels. A river sparkled beside the path, so clear it reflected the clouds like a mirror. Trees with thick green leaves stretched their arms over the water, casting cool shadows. Every branch was heavy with fruit that somehow looked both refreshing and magical—apples, peaches, grapes, and fruits they couldn't even name.

Christian cupped his hands and dipped them into the river. He took a sip. Cold, sweet water filled his mouth, and something shifted inside—his exhaustion melted, replaced by a quiet strength. "This... this is the River of Life," he whispered.

Hopeful knelt beside him and drank too. His eyes lit up. "It's like... joy, in liquid form."

They wandered along the riverbank for a while, breathing in the fresh air scented with flowers and something sweet, like honey. The trees gave shade without being gloomy. The grass was soft, dotted with lilies and wildflowers, green and full even though it had been a long journey.

"This is what we needed," Christian said, sitting down again. "Rest that actually restores."

"I could stay here forever," Hopeful admitted, pulling an apple from a low branch. It was the best thing he'd ever tasted.

They ate, drank, and eventually stretched out on the meadow to sleep. There were no fears here. No voices of discouragement. Just peace. It wrapped around them like a blanket.

Day after day, they returned to the fruit and the river, letting it refill the places in their souls that had run dry. They sang softly, sometimes aloud, sometimes just in their hearts, songs of gratitude. Songs of joy. Songs of awe.

"Whoever finds this place," Christian murmured one night, "will trade everything to have it. This field, this river... it's worth everything."

Hopeful nodded. "But we can't stay. The journey isn't over."

Christian smiled. "No. But we leave stronger than when we came."

And with that, they shouldered their packs, took one last drink from the River of Life, and stepped forward, refreshed, ready, and full of hope.

Teen Commentary

Why Rest Isn't a Waste

Let's be real—sometimes life feels like a *nonstop* treadmill. School. Sports. Drama. Doubts. Pressure to be perfect. Even your faith journey can start to feel like another checklist.

That's why this scene hits so hard.

Christian and Hopeful didn't just crash by accident. They were *given* rest—on purpose. God built it into their journey.

And guess what? That's for you too. Rest isn't laziness. It's a gift. A way for your heart, mind, and soul to *breathe* again. And that "River of Life"? That's Jesus. His presence refreshes your spirit in ways no vacation, binge-watch, or iced coffee ever could.

The world says, "Hustle harder." God says, "Come to Me... and rest." (See Matthew 11:28–30.)

So maybe you don't need to do *more* today. Maybe you just need to come sit by the river.

Reflection Questions

1. When was the last time you truly rested—not just physically, but spiritually or emotionally?

2. What helps *you* feel closer to God when you're overwhelmed or burned out?

3. Why do you think we sometimes feel guilty about slowing down?

4. What might it look like for you to "drink from the River of Life" in your everyday life?

Scripture Connection

"He makes me lie down in green pastures. He leads me beside still waters. He restores my soul."—*Psalm 23:2–3 (ESV)*

Devotional Prayer

God, thank You for inviting me to rest—not just to stop moving, but to be refreshed by Your presence. Help me pause when I need it, not just push through. Fill me again with peace, joy, and strength that only You can give. I want to walk with You, not just for You. Remind me that I'm loved even when I'm not "doing" anything. Teach me to rest well, so I can live well. Amen.

Scene 31

BY-PATH MEADOW

The sky was still bright when Christian and Hopeful left the river behind. The peaceful waters they had walked beside for so long veered off in another direction, and the path ahead turned rocky and rough. Their feet—already sore and blistered—ached with every step, and their hearts sank.

"This kinda sucks," Christian muttered, kicking a stone.

Hopeful nodded, eyes scanning the path ahead. "Feels like it's getting harder."

"I just wish there was an easier way," Christian sighed, brushing sweat off his brow.

As if on cue, a break in the fence to their left caught his eye. A small wooden stile led into a wide green field. The grass was soft, the ground level, and—most importantly—a path ran through it parallel to their own.

"Hopeful," Christian called, "look at this! The meadow runs right along our route. If we go over this stile, we'll still be heading the same direction—but on smoother ground."

Hopeful hesitated. "But what if that path leads somewhere else?"

Christian leaned against the fence, pointing. "It's literally right beside ours. Same direction. Same destination. Come on—it'll be way easier."

Hopeful still looked unsure, but followed his friend over the stile.

And at first? It was awesome. The grass cushioned every step. The wind was cool. Even the path seemed to smile beneath their feet.

Up ahead, they spotted a man walking confidently.

"Hey!" Christian called. "Where does this path lead?"

The man turned, flashing a wide grin. "To the Celestial City, of course!"

Christian elbowed Hopeful with a "See? Told you so" look, and the two sped up to follow. The man's name, they would later learn, was Vain-Confidence.

But as the sun dipped low, things changed. Clouds rolled in. The air turned heavy. The path twisted. The man ahead faded into the growing darkness.

Then—suddenly—they heard it.

A scream. A crash. Silence.

"Hello?" Christian called out, heart racing.

No response. Just groaning. Then—nothing.

Hopeful's voice trembled. "Where... where are we?"

Christian was silent.

The rain started slow—then came in sheets. Lightning split the sky. The path turned to mud. Water rushed in around their ankles.

"I should've said no," Hopeful groaned. "I *knew* this was a bad idea."

Christian winced. "I didn't mean to lead you wrong. I thought it would be okay. I'm so sorry."

Hopeful nodded, rain streaking his face. "I forgive you. Let's just get out of here."

Christian stepped forward. "Let me go first."

"No," Hopeful said firmly. "You're upset. If danger comes again, you might panic. I'll lead."

And just when it felt like all hope was drowning, a voice echoed through the storm—clear and steady:

"Set your heart back on the highway. Return."

It gave them the courage to turn around, even though every step back was harder than the one before. The water was waist-deep. They nearly drowned more than once. But soaked, exhausted, and shaking—they made it.

Teen Commentary

Shortcut Regrets & Stormy Roads

Ever wish life had a fast-forward button? Or maybe a shortcut to avoid all the hard stuff—awkward conversations, boring responsibilities, painful moments?

Christian and Hopeful *literally* saw an easier path and thought, "Why not?" It *looked* like it led the right way. It even had someone confidently leading the charge. But confidence doesn't equal truth. And shortcuts that look spiritual can still pull you off track.

This scene is a wake-up call. Even strong Christians can wander. Even well-meaning friends can lead us wrong. But the beautiful part? Grace meets us in our mistakes. Forgiveness and humility restore friendship. And God—even in thunder and flood—still speaks:

"Come back. You're not too far gone."

Let's be real: life will get stormy. But the right path isn't always the smoothest—it's the one that leads you closer to Jesus.

Reflection Questions

1. Have you ever taken a shortcut in life or faith that ended up leading you further away from God?

2. Why do you think it's so tempting to follow people who seem confident, even if we're unsure of their direction?

3. How do you respond when someone gently challenges your choices?

4. Is there a part of your life where you hear God saying, "Come back"?

Scripture Connection

"Set up road signs; put up guideposts. Mark well the path by which you came. Come back again…" —*Jeremiah 31:21 (NLT)*

Devotional Prayer

Heavenly Father, I admit—sometimes I chase the easy path instead of the right one. Thank You for calling me back when I mess up. Help me listen to wise counsel, lead with humility, and trust You even when the road is hard. In Jesus' Name, Amen.

Scene 32

GIANT DESPAIR: TRAPPED IN DOUBTING CASTLE

The sky had gone steel-gray, and rain drizzled like it had no intention of stopping. Christian and Hopeful had lost the path hours ago, slipping over a stile in the fence because it *looked* like a shortcut. It wasn't.

By the time they realized their mistake, night was choking out the last light. Exhausted, soaked, and discouraged, they stumbled into a clump of trees, leaned against each other, and passed out under the faint shelter of branches.

They didn't know it, but they had wandered into the property of Doubting Castle.

The next morning, the earth trembled under something massive. Heavy, booted feet stomped toward them. Christian's eyes shot open as a shadow fell over him.

"Hey!" growled a deep, booming voice. "What do you think you're doing on *my* land?"

Standing over them was a towering man, thick as a wall and twice as angry. His face looked like it had forgotten how to smile. This was Giant Despair.

"Uh—we—we're pilgrims," Hopeful stammered, trying to stand. "We got lost. We didn't mean to—"

"You *trespassed*," the Giant snarled. "And now… you're mine."

They didn't even try to run. He grabbed them with hands like concrete blocks and dragged them through the mud to a stone fortress surrounded by thorny hedges. Inside, he shoved them into a pitch-black dungeon that stank of rot and sorrow. Then he slammed the door and left them in darkness.

For days, no one came. No food. No water. Just silence—except for the whispers of despair inside their minds.

"This is all my fault," Christian groaned one evening, curled in a corner. "I led us here. We should've never taken that path. We're going to die in here."

Hopeful was quiet, his face pale. "I don't know what to say."

On the third day, the dungeon door creaked open. Despair's silhouette loomed.

"My wife thinks I should beat you again," he said flatly. "I think she's right."

He stepped in and brought a thick club down on them—once, twice, over and over. Christian crumpled, gasping. Hopeful couldn't move. The Giant finally left them there, bleeding and broken.

The next day, he returned again. "You'll never escape. This will be your grave. Why not end it yourselves? I can give you a knife… or a rope. It'll be better than this."

Then he smiled.

The door shut.

Christian pressed his forehead against the cold wall. "Maybe he's right," he whispered. "This is no life. We're nothing but failures."

"No," Hopeful said weakly, eyes shining with tears but steady. "No, Christian. Listen to me."

Christian turned.

"I've thought about it too," Hopeful admitted. "But God says, 'You shall not murder.' That includes ourselves. We can't give up. We're not the first to be here—and some have made it out. What if this isn't the end? What if God still has a way?"

Christian didn't answer, but something stirred inside him.

Later that night, they heard the Giant and his wife talking.

"They're too stubborn," Despair grumbled. "Maybe they're holding onto hope. Or maybe they have… a way out."

He laughed.

At midnight, Christian and Hopeful lay side by side in the dark.

"We should pray," Hopeful whispered.

So they did. Long and hard. Words spilled out like water, desperate and raw. They poured their hearts out to God, right there in the dirt.

Then Christian sat up sharply. "Wait."

Hopeful blinked at him. "What?"

"I'm such an idiot," Christian said, patting his chest. "I forgot—I have a key. It's called *Promise*. I've had it this whole time. I think… I think it can open the door!"

Hopeful's eyes widened. "Well, what are you waiting for? Try it!"

Christian scrambled to the lock, shoved the key in. *Click.* The bolt moved. The door opened.

They bolted from the cell, rushing down the corridor. The yard door—*click.* The gate—stuck for a second, then opened with a shriek that echoed through the castle.

"RUN!" Christian yelled.

Behind them, Despair roared in fury. But as he tried to chase them, he staggered and collapsed, clutching his chest. A sudden fit overtook him, and he couldn't move.

The two friends tore through the field and climbed over the stile, breathless and shaking, but free. They were finally out of Doubting Castle.

That day, they carved a warning in a stone nearby:

"This is the way to Doubting Castle—guarded by Giant Despair. Beware."

Teen Commentary

Don't Stay in the Dungeon

Ever felt stuck in your own version of a dungeon? Maybe you made a bad choice. Maybe you're overwhelmed, ashamed, or just plain tired. That's exactly where Christian and Hopeful ended up—lost, hurting, and ready to give up. And guess what? That's exactly where Despair loves to trap people.

But here's the crazy thing: *Christian already had the key the whole time*. It was the Promise of God. He just forgot.

God's promises don't vanish when you're in the dark. They're still there—unchanged, still powerful. Sometimes it takes prayer, a friend, and a moment of clarity to remember: *You don't have to stay trapped.*

Hopeful didn't give in—and because of that, neither did Christian. Never underestimate the power of encouraging someone who's ready to quit.

Reflection Questions

1. Have you ever felt trapped in a "dungeon" of doubt, fear, or shame? What helped you get out—or what's keeping you stuck?

2. What "keys" (like Scripture, prayer, or godly friends) has God already given you that you might be forgetting right now?

3. What kind of influence are you when a friend is in despair—do you pull them deeper, or point them toward hope?

4. Why do you think Satan uses despair and hopelessness to keep Christians from moving forward?

Scripture Connection

"Why, my soul, are you downcast? Why so disturbed within me? Put your hope in God, for I will yet praise him, my Savior and my God."
—*Psalm 42:11 (NIV)*

Devotional Prayer

Heavenly Father, when I feel trapped in darkness, remind me that Your promises still hold. Help me not to forget the truth in the middle of pain. Give me the courage to pray, the strength to wait, and the hope to try again. And if someone I know is struggling, help me be like Hopeful— a friend who points to You. In Jesus' Name, Amen.

THE DELECTABLE MOUNTAINS

The trail had been long—muddy, rocky, and relentless. Christian and Hopeful were exhausted. Their legs ached, and their spirits were drained. But as they crested a rise, their eyes widened.

Stretching before them was a breathtaking landscape: lush hills rolling under a golden sky, gardens bursting with fruit, fountains bubbling with crystal-clear water. Birds sang overhead, and the air carried a peaceful hush, like heaven had touched earth.

Christian let out a low whistle. "This must be the place. The Delectable Mountains."

Hopeful's eyes sparkled. "After everything… it feels like we've finally found rest."

As they wandered deeper, they noticed shepherds standing by the roadside. They were old, but strong-looking—each face calm, eyes wise. They stood like people who'd seen things… deep things.

Christian stepped forward, leaning on his staff. "Hey, can I ask— whose mountains are these? And the sheep—who do they belong to?"

One of the shepherds smiled, his beard rustling in the breeze. "This is Immanuel's Land. The sheep? They're His. He gave His life for them."

Christian's voice softened. "Is this the way to the Celestial City?"

"You're on the right path," another shepherd nodded.

"How far is it?" Hopeful asked, eyes searching the horizon.

The shepherd named Knowledge answered, "Far. But only those truly meant to reach it will make it."

Christian glanced at Hopeful. "Is the road safe?"

The shepherd named Watchful stepped forward. "For the faithful? Yes. But those who rebel… they fall."

The two pilgrims exchanged a quiet, serious look. Then Hopeful asked, "We're tired. Is there a place here where we can rest?"

"Of course," said the shepherd named Sincere. "Our Lord told us to always welcome pilgrims. Come—eat, drink, rest."

That night, after a full meal and warm hospitality, the shepherds sat around the fire with Christian and Hopeful.

"You've come far," said the shepherd named Experience. "Not many do."

Hopeful nodded. "It's been rough. But God's helped us keep going."

The shepherds looked at one another and smiled. "Welcome to the Delectable Mountains," they said in unison.

The Next Morning: Lessons on the Mountain

The next morning, the shepherds invited them for a walk.

"We want to show you some things," said Knowledge. "Things that will help you finish the journey."

They first climbed a hill called *Error*. When they looked over the edge, Christian stepped back, his stomach turning. At the bottom were shattered bodies.

"What happened to them?" he asked.

"They followed false teachers," said Watchful. "They climbed too high in pride and fell. Let it be a warning—don't mess with distorted truth."

Next was a hill called *Caution*. Far off, they saw people stumbling blindly among tombstones.

"They once were pilgrims, like you," said Sincere. "But when the path got hard, they took a shortcut. It led to Doubting Castle, where Giant Despair blinded them. Now they wander, lost."

Hopeful's hands clenched. "That could've been us…"

Then the shepherds led them to a hill with a dark hole in the side. "This is a byway to hell," said Experience gravely. "Some looked the part of pilgrims but sold out the truth, lived for lies, and now… this is their end."

Hopeful shivered. "They went so far… and still fell?"

"Yes," said Knowledge. "Some made it even past this mountain. But they lacked real strength, real commitment."

Christian whispered, "We need to ask God for strength every day."

"Amen," said the shepherds. "And use it when it's given."

Finally, the shepherds took them to a high hill called *Clear*. They handed them a special telescope.

"If your eyes are steady," said Watchful, "you'll catch a glimpse of the Celestial City."

Christian tried, but his hands were still shaking from what he had seen. Still, through blurry eyes, he thought he saw a faraway city glowing in the sunlight.

He whispered, "Hopeful... do you see it?"

Hopeful nodded slowly. "Just barely. But it's there."

The shepherds smiled and sang a quiet song:

"The Shepherds show what others miss,

The hidden things, the truths, the bliss.

Come near and see what lies ahead—

The life beyond, for which you've bled."

As the pilgrims left, each shepherd gave them a parting word:

- "Here's a map—follow it closely."
- "Beware of smooth talkers."
- "Don't fall asleep on enchanted ground."
- "Godspeed."

And with that, Christian and Hopeful walked on.

Teen Commentary

Let's be real—life can feel like a grind. But then, boom! You hit one of those moments where you feel God's presence so clearly it stops you in your tracks. That's the Delectable Mountains.

This scene is all about resting without quitting, learning without zoning out, and seeing what's really at stake. Christian and Hopeful are refreshed, but they're also warned. Not every journey that *starts* with Jesus ends at Heaven if we bail out, check out, or fake it.

The Shepherds? They're like the wise mentors or youth leaders in your life—people God uses to give you insight, encouragement, and correction. Lean in. Listen. Learn.

God doesn't just want you to survive the Christian life—He wants you to thrive with eyes wide open, heart anchored in truth, and your gaze fixed on the Celestial City.

Reflection Questions

1. Have you ever had a "Delectable Mountain" moment—where you felt close to God or refreshed in your faith?

2. What shortcuts or temptations sometimes try to pull you off God's path?

3. Which shepherd (Knowledge, Watchful, Experience, Sincere) do you need more of in your life right now?

4. How can you help others stay on the path when they're struggling?

Scripture Connection

"Let us not become weary in doing good, for at the proper time we will reap a harvest if we do not give up."—*Galatians 6:9 (NIV)*

Devotional Prayer

Heavenly Father, thank You for places of rest and people of wisdom. Help me to stay alert on the journey, not just enjoying the view but learning the lessons You're showing me. Protect me from shortcuts that lead to despair, and keep my eyes fixed on You and the eternal hope I have in Christ. Give me strength—not just to believe, but to finish strong. In Jesus' Name, Amen.

Scene 34

IGNORANCE FROM CONCEIT

Christian and Hopeful had just finished the descent from the mountain peaks, where the air was clean and the Shepherds had refreshed their hearts. Now the road flattened out, winding like a path through a quiet valley.

The sun was warm. The breeze was calm. For a while, the two friends walked in silence, soaking in the peace.

Then, from a narrow, crooked trail that split off from the main road, a teenaged guy about their age stepped out and started walking confidently alongside them. He wore clean clothes, had good posture, and moved with the energy of someone who thought he knew exactly where he was going.

"Hey," Christian said, catching his eye. "Where are you from?"

The guy smiled. "A place just down that way," he said, pointing toward the crooked trail. "It's called Conceit. I'm heading to the Celestial City."

Christian and Hopeful exchanged a glance. "Wait," Christian asked cautiously, "how do you plan to get through the gate?"

Ignorance shrugged like it was a dumb question. "Same way as everyone else. I'm a good person. I do what's right. I pray. I give to charity. I've never done anything *that* bad."

"But," Christian pressed gently, "did you come through the narrow gate at the beginning of the road? The one by the cross?"

"Nah," Ignorance said, waving it off. "That's the long way. Nobody in my country even knows how to find that gate. Our lane connects to this road just fine, and it's actually nicer than the one you're on."

Hopeful raised an eyebrow. "You sure you're on the right path? Like, really sure?"

Ignorance looked at them like they were crazy. "Look, you guys do your religion your way, and I'll do mine. As long as we're all sincere, it'll work out. Besides, God knows my heart."

Christian's jaw tightened. "But He also knows if someone's trying to skip the part where they surrender."

Ignorance chuckled and walked a little faster. "Okay, well… good luck with all that."

As he walked ahead, Christian leaned toward Hopeful. "There's more hope for a fool than for someone who thinks he's too smart for truth."

Hopeful nodded solemnly. "Let's give him some space. Maybe the things we said will stick with him later."

They walked in silence again—until the sky seemed to dim.

The road turned into a dark, twisting lane. Fog hovered near the ground. Shadows moved like they were alive.

Suddenly, out of the darkness, they saw something that made their blood run cold.

A man was being dragged down the path by invisible chains. His face was pale. His eyes empty. Seven dark, shadowy figures—devils—surrounded him, pulling him toward a black door embedded in the side of a hill. On his back was a glowing label:

"Fake Believer. Rejected. Apostate."

Christian froze. "I think I know him... I think that was Turn-Away, from the town of Apostasy."

Hopeful trembled. "That's what happens when someone pretends to follow God but never truly gives Him their heart."

They stood in silence as the shadows faded into the mist.

And they prayed quietly that they would never end up like him—or like Ignorance, who thought the journey didn't need the truth.

Teen Commentary

Truth Isn't Optional

This scene hits different.

Ignorance is that guy who thinks he's good enough on his own—he's doing *all the right things*, but never surrendered his heart. He skipped the cross, skipped the narrow gate, and thinks being "nice" is enough.

Christian and Hopeful try to warn him, but he brushes them off like he's too smart to listen. Ever met someone like that? Maybe… been someone like that?

Then there's the guy getting dragged away—Turn-Away. His story is a warning that even people who *look* like believers on the outside can fall if they never truly gave their lives to Jesus.

Being religious isn't the same as being rescued.

Looking good isn't the same as living in truth.

Jesus is the only way. Not our performance. Not our good vibes. Just Him.

Reflection Questions

1. Have you ever tried to "shortcut" your relationship with God—doing the right stuff without giving Him your heart?

2. What's the difference between "being a good person" and being a true follower of Jesus?

3. Do you know someone who might be like Ignorance—confident, but lost? How could you lovingly talk to them?

4. What are some signs in your life that your faith is real, not just surface-level?

Scripture Connection

"There is a way that seems right to a man, but its end is the way to death."—*Proverbs 14:12 (ESV)*

Devotional Prayer

Heavenly Father, it's easy to trust myself—to think I've got this, that I'm good enough, that You'll accept me because I try hard. But I see now that none of that works without You. Save me from pride, from fake religion, and from shortcuts that avoid the cross. Help me to follow You fully and live in truth—even when it's hard. I don't want to just look the part. I want to be Yours. In Jesus' Name, Amen.

THE STORY OF LITTLE-FAITH

The sun had just dipped beneath the trees when Little-Faith wandered into a narrow, eerie alley called Deadman's Lane. The name alone should've made him turn back—but he was tired. His sneakers were caked in mud, his hoodie torn, and his backpack felt heavier than ever. He had come from the town of Sincere, determined to stay on the King's path toward the Celestial City.

But right now, all he wanted was to sit. Just for a second.

He plopped down on a half-broken bench and drifted into a restless sleep.

Suddenly—

"Yo! Get up!"

Little-Faith's eyes shot open. Three guys stood over him, their faces shadowed under hoodies. One had a chain wrapped around his fist. Another had ink-black eyes and a smug grin. The third guy—tall and silent—held a thick wooden bat. They weren't just random bullies.

They were Faint-Heart, Mistrust, and Guilt.

Little-Faith's stomach dropped.

"Stand up," Faint-Heart barked, shoving him with his foot. "Hand over your cash."

"I... I don't want trouble," Little-Faith stammered, trying to stand. His hands shook as he fumbled with his backpack.

"Too slow," said Mistrust, yanking the bag from his back. "Let's see what this little pilgrim's hiding."

"Thieves!" Little-Faith yelled, but his voice cracked in fear.

Before he could run, Guilt raised the bat and *crack!*—everything went black.

When he came to, they were gone. His money was too. He staggered to his feet, head throbbing, heart heavier than ever. His special items—his "jewels," proof of his citizenship in the Kingdom—were still tucked away, unnoticed by the thieves. But his spending money? Gone. He barely had enough to get through the rest of the trip.

As Little-Faith limped back onto the path, he felt ashamed. Angry. Hurt. Why hadn't he fought back? Why hadn't he seen them coming?

He trudged on, often hungry, often begging. And every time he felt a flicker of hope—remembering that his jewels were still safe—shame would whisper, *But look how weak you were. Look what you lost.*

He told his story to anyone who'd listen. Over and over again. Where it happened. How it happened. What he lost. And though he kept moving, his heart stayed stuck in Deadman's Lane.

Teen Commentary

The Struggle Is Real

Okay, let's be real—this story *hurts*. Little-Faith was a good guy. He was doing the right thing, staying on the right path... and *still* got wrecked. It wasn't some epic battle either—he didn't have the strength, the confidence, or the fight in him. He got jumped. Just like that.

Ever been there?

Maybe it's not a literal alley, but more like a season—when your faith feels small, your hope feels stolen, and you wonder if you'll ever feel whole again. You still believe... but you're tired. And maybe ashamed.

But here's the thing: *Little-Faith kept walking*. Even though he limped. Even though he was broke. Even though he felt like a failure. He didn't sell his soul or give up his identity, even when it would've been easier.

That's strength too. Quiet strength. The kind that survives.

And hey, the enemy didn't get his most valuable stuff—his ID, his jewels. That's no accident. That's *grace*.

Reflection Questions

1. Have you ever felt spiritually "jumped"—like life hit you hard and left your faith shaken? What helped you keep going?

2. What are your "jewels"—the unshakeable parts of your identity in Christ that no one can steal?

3. How do shame or guilt sometimes keep you stuck, even when you know you're still on the right path?

4. What does "faith" look like when it's little—but still real?

Scripture Connection

"We are pressed on every side by troubles, but we are not crushed. We are perplexed, but not driven to despair. We are hunted down, but never abandoned by God. We get knocked down, but we are not destroyed." —*2 Corinthians 4:8–9 (NLT)*

Devotional Prayer

Heavenly Father, sometimes I feel like Little-Faith—overwhelmed, embarrassed, and unsure if I can keep going. Thank You that even when I'm weak, You don't let go of me. Remind me of the treasures You've placed in my heart that can never be stolen. Help me walk forward, even with a limp. Give me grace for the journey, and courage to keep trusting You—especially when I feel broken. In Jesus' Name, Amen.

Scene 36

THE FLATTERER

Christian and Hopeful walked down the dusty trail, the sun dipping lower in the sky, casting long shadows behind them. They were tired but focused, the glowing Celestial City still clear in their hearts, if not their eyes.

A little ways ahead, the road split.

"Wait... this can't be right," Christian said, stopping. "There's two paths now?"

Hopeful squinted. Both roads looked basically identical—same smooth ground, same winding curves disappearing into the distance.

"Which one leads to the City?" Hopeful asked, pulling out a crumpled paper from his pocket. It was the map the shepherds had given them back on the Delectable Mountains. But he hesitated. "I think... I think we'll be fine without it."

Christian nodded slowly, folding his arms. "Yeah. They both look the same anyway."

Just then, a man approached. He wore glowing white robes that shimmered under the sun, but something about his walk felt... off. Smooth. Too smooth.

"You two look confused," the man said, his voice like honey. "Lost?"

"We're heading to the Celestial City," Christian replied. "But we're unsure which road to take."

"Oh, that's easy," the man said with a warm smile. "I'm headed there myself. Follow me—I know the way better than anyone."

Hopeful looked at Christian. Christian shrugged. The man *seemed* legit, and he looked the part. Confident. Holy. Glowing even.

So they followed.

At first, the road seemed fine. But slowly—almost without realizing it—the path curved. Then curved more. Until they weren't facing toward the mountains anymore.

"Hey," Hopeful said, frowning, "I think we've turned around..."

Before Christian could respond, the ground gave way beneath them.

Snap!

A thick, invisible net sprang up around them, tangling their arms and legs. They crashed to the dirt in a mess of limbs and panic.

"What is this?!" Christian yelled.

The man's white robe slipped off—and underneath, he was clothed in black. His eyes, no longer gentle, sparkled with mockery. He disappeared into the shadows, leaving them trapped.

Hopeful groaned. "We should've read the note. The shepherds *warned* us about this."

Christian pounded the ground. "They said to watch out for the Flatterer. We were *literally* warned. Proverbs even says it: 'A man who flatters his neighbor spreads a net for his feet.' That's us. In a net."

For a while, they just sat there, stuck, miserable, and silent. Finally, a bright light began to grow on the path. A figure—shining like the sun—walked toward them. He held a whip, but his eyes were full of truth and love.

"What happened here?" he asked, arms crossed.

They confessed everything. The road. The man. The net. The robe.

"That was the Flatterer," the shining one said firmly. "A deceiver. A false apostle pretending to be good."

He ripped the net open with one quick motion, and the two pilgrims stumbled out, bruised and humbled.

"Where did you stay last night?" he asked.

"With the shepherds," Christian answered.

"Did they give you instructions?"

"Yes…"

"Did you read them when you got confused?"

Christian and Hopeful looked down. "No. We forgot."

The shining one sighed. "Didn't they also warn you about the Flatterer?"

Hopeful nodded. "We didn't think it was him. He looked… perfect."

The shining one looked at them with sadness and love. "Flatterers deceive with charm. But you must know the truth for yourself."

Then he commanded them to lie down. "This will hurt," he said, "but it will teach you."

He disciplined them—firmly, but not cruelly. It stung, but something inside them healed too. Their pride. Their carelessness.

"As many as I love," he said, "I rebuke and discipline. Be zealous, and repent."

When it was over, he helped them up. "Now go. Stay on the right path. And this time—read your directions."

They nodded, sore but wiser. And as they walked forward—this time slowly, carefully—they sang a quiet tune under their breath, a song of caution and grace.

Teen Commentary

Ever met someone who seemed to have all the right words... but the wrong direction?

Christian and Hopeful totally fell for it. Why? Because the Flatterer didn't *look* wrong. He talked sweet. He acted spiritual. But his goal was to trap them.

Real talk: life is full of flattering voices—people, influencers, even thoughts—that sound good but twist your path away from what's true. Sometimes they say what you *want* to hear, not what you *need* to hear. That's why Christian and Hopeful fell—because they didn't check their map (a.k.a. the truth they already had).

But here's the good news: even after they messed up, they weren't abandoned. God disciplines not to destroy—but to redirect.

He rescues *and* corrects.

That's love.

Reflection Questions

1. Have you ever followed someone's advice or influence that seemed good at first but led you in the wrong direction?

2. Why do you think flattery is so effective? What makes it dangerous?

3. What "maps" has God given you (like Scripture, wise mentors, prayer) that you sometimes forget to check?

4. What's one way you can grow in recognizing truth vs. deception in your daily life?

Scripture Connection

"A man who flatters his neighbor spreads a net for his feet."—*Proverbs 29:5 (ESV)*

Devotional Prayer

Heavenly Father, help me to see clearly when the path looks confusing. Give me discernment when someone's words sound nice but aren't true. Help me remember the directions You've given me—through Your Word, through mentors, through Your Spirit. And when I mess up, please correct me with love and bring me back to You. I want to walk Your way, even when it's hard. In Jesus' Name, Amen.

Scene 37

THE ATHEIST

Christian and Hopeful were walking along a dusty road beneath the blazing afternoon sun. Their backpacks were lighter now—trials and detours had stripped away many burdens—but their minds were still alert. Every shadow seemed like it could hold a test.

"Hey, you see that guy up ahead?" Christian asked, shading his eyes. A lone man was walking toward them slowly, head down, hands stuffed in his hoodie pocket. "He's walking *away* from Mount Zion."

Hopeful squinted. "Yeah… we should be careful. What if he's another Flatterer in disguise?"

The man finally approached. He was older, with tired eyes and a mocking smirk. He looked them up and down like they were wearing clown costumes.

"Where you two headed?" he asked, one eyebrow raised.

"We're on our way to Mount Zion," Christian replied, standing tall.

Atheist snorted. Then he burst out laughing—a deep, cynical laugh that made Christian and Hopeful exchange a glance.

"Wait, *you're serious?*" the man chuckled. "That's rich. You're wasting your time. There's no such place."

Christian frowned. "Why would you say that?"

"Because I've looked!" the man snapped, suddenly serious. "I left my home twenty years ago chasing the same dream you're on. I gave up everything to find this so-called 'City of God.' Guess what? It doesn't exist. You're better off turning back now, like I am."

Christian looked at Hopeful, uncertain. "What if he's right? He's gone farther than we have."

Hopeful stepped forward, fire in his eyes. "Don't even think about it. We've already been tricked once, remember? We saw the gates of the city from the mountains! We walk by faith, not by sight. This guy—he gave up. But we *believe*."

The man rolled his eyes. "Suit yourselves. When you've walked as long as I have, and the road keeps going nowhere, you'll understand."

Christian faced the man. "I didn't ask because I doubted—I asked to see what was in my brother's heart. And now I know. As for you, your eyes are blinded by lies. But we know the truth."

Hopeful smiled. "And the truth gives hope."

The two travelers turned away, leaving the Atheist behind in the dust. He chuckled to himself and wandered off, back toward the world.

But Christian and Hopeful walked forward, shoulders squared, faith stronger than ever.

Teen Commentary

Don't Let Doubt Derail You

Ever been made fun of for your faith? Or maybe heard someone say, "Christianity is just a fairy tale for weak people"? Yeah—this scene hits home. Christian and Hopeful meet someone who once believed, but gave up when the journey didn't go how he expected.

Atheist had the facts, but not the faith. He walked the walk for years but stopped trusting the destination. His laughter wasn't joy—it was bitterness.

Sometimes, people who walk away from God will try to convince you to do the same. Why? Because if they gave up, they want others to give up too—it makes them feel less alone in their decision.

But here's the deal: following Jesus *isn't* always easy or popular. You might not "see" immediate results. But that doesn't mean the destination isn't real. Faith isn't blind—faith is trusting what you *know* to be true even when you can't see it yet.

Christian and Hopeful stayed on the path because they remembered the truth, and they reminded *each other*. That's why walking with strong, faithful friends matters. When doubt whispers—or screams—you need someone who won't let you stop believing.

Reflection Questions

1. Have you ever felt tempted to give up on your faith because it felt hard, lonely, or pointless?

2. What are some "voices" in your life (people, media, influencers) that make you question if faith is worth it?

3. How can you build a stronger friendship with someone who encourages your walk with God like Hopeful did?

4. If you could talk to someone like Atheist, what would you say to show them hope isn't dead?

Scripture Connection

"But we are not of those who shrink back and are destroyed, but of those who have faith and preserve their souls."— *Hebrews 10:39 (ESV)*

Devotional Prayer

Heavenly Father, sometimes the road feels long and uncertain. I hear voices that tell me to turn back, to give up, to stop trusting You. But deep down, I know You are real, and I know You are good. Help me walk by faith, even when I can't see. Strengthen my heart. Surround me with people who help me believe. And when doubt comes, remind me of Your truth. I choose to keep going, eyes on You. In Jesus' Name, Amen.

Scene 38

THE ENCHANTED GROUND

The sun was dipping low, washing everything in golden haze as Christian and Hopeful trudged forward along the trail. The path had been hard, but something about this stretch of road was… different. The air was warm—too warm—and the breeze had a lazy, lulling hum to it, like a lullaby whispered in the leaves. Even the trees drooped as if they were falling asleep.

Hopeful blinked slowly and let out a yawn.

"Bro, I can barely keep my eyes open," he muttered, dragging his feet. "This place is like a giant sleep spell. Let's just stop here and rest for a bit. Just for a few minutes."

Christian turned sharply. "No way. Don't even think about it."

"C'mon," Hopeful insisted, rubbing his eyes. "We've been walking forever. A quick nap won't kill us."

Christian's voice tightened. "Actually, it *might*. Don't you remember what the Shepherds told us? This is the Enchanted Ground. People fall asleep here… and never wake up."

Hopeful froze. "Right. I forgot."

Christian stepped closer, clapping a firm hand on his shoulder. "We've got to stay awake. Spiritually and literally. Let's talk. Keep each other sharp."

Hopeful gave a sheepish smile. "Thanks, man. If I was here alone, I probably would've passed out by now."

"Yeah," Christian nodded, "Two are better than one."

They kept walking, shaking off the drowsiness by talking. Hopeful spoke honestly about his journey, about how he once chased everything the world promised—money, parties, fake friendships, and temporary highs. "Back then, I didn't care about God," he said. "I mean, I *knew* about Him, but sin just felt… fun. Like, too good to give up."

Christian nodded slowly. "So what changed?"

Hopeful kicked a rock down the path. "Honestly? Fear. I started noticing things—like, a friend would get sick, or I'd hear someone died suddenly, and it would hit me: I'm not invincible. I'm gonna die one day. And I'm not ready."

He paused, looking at Christian. "I tried to clean up my life. You know—read the Bible, pray, stop partying. I thought maybe if I just became a good person, I'd be safe."

"And did that work?" Christian asked gently.

Hopeful shook his head. "Nope. Because even when I tried to do good, I saw how messed up I still was. My thoughts, my pride, my selfishness… it was like sin was baked into everything I did."

Christian raised an eyebrow. "So what did you do?"

"I opened up to Faithful," Hopeful said, his voice softening. "He told me I needed *someone else's* righteousness—someone perfect. That's when I heard about Jesus. Not just the Sunday School version—but the real One. The only One who never sinned. Who traded His perfection for my mess."

Christian smiled. "That's the only hope any of us have."

The two friends walked on, awake and alert, sharing stories, reminding each other of truth. And in the middle of the Enchanted Ground—where so many others had dozed off and disappeared—they stayed wide awake, fueled by real conversation and the hope that only Christ could give.

Teen Commentary

Have you ever felt spiritually sleepy? Like you're just coasting through life, scrolling, zoning out, not really thinking deeply about anything that matters?

That's exactly what *The Enchanted Ground* is. It's not about physical sleep—it's about spiritual sleep. The kind that sneaks in when you stop caring, stop growing, stop praying, stop thinking about where you're headed.

Hopeful was tempted to "just take a nap." And let's be real—how often do we *check out* spiritually because we're bored, tired, or distracted by things that seem more fun or more urgent? That's why Christian said no. He knew it was dangerous. Deadly, even.

But what kept them awake? *Talking honestly. Telling their stories. Encouraging each other.* That's how we fight spiritual sleep. Not by being perfect, but by staying in community and focusing on Jesus.

Reflection Questions

1. What "Enchanted Grounds" are you facing right now—places or habits that make you spiritually lazy or distracted?

2. When have you tried to "clean up your life" without really depending on Jesus?

3. Who in your life helps you stay spiritually awake? Who could *you* help?

4. How can sharing your story—like Hopeful did—help someone else stay awake in their faith?

Scripture Connection

"So then, let us not be like others, who are asleep, but let us be awake and sober."— *1 Thessalonians 5:6 (NIV)*

Devotional Prayer

Heavenly Father, sometimes I get tired. Not just physically, but spiritually. I zone out, I drift, I chase after things that don't matter. Wake me up. Help me stay alert, especially in the places where it's easy to fall asleep in my faith. Give me friends who speak truth to me—and help me be that kind of friend too. Thank You for being the one who never sleeps and never lets go. Keep me walking with You, eyes open and heart alive. In Jesus' Name, Amen.

Scene 39

IGNORANCE DEMONSTRATES HIS IGNORANCE

The gravel crunched under Christian's boots as he walked beside Hopeful down the narrow path, the late afternoon sun casting long shadows through the trees. Birds chirped lazily, and the wind tugged at their clothes like a playful child. It was the kind of peaceful stretch that invited deep conversation—except Hopeful kept glancing behind them.

"Hey, look," Hopeful said, tilting his head toward the bend in the trail. "That guy—Ignorance, right?—he's way behind. Just strolling like he's got all day."

Christian didn't even bother turning around. "Yeah, I saw. He clearly doesn't care about walking with us."

Hopeful shrugged. "Still, I don't see how it would've hurt him to keep up."

Christian smirked. "He probably thinks he's better off without us."

"Probably. But let's wait up anyway."

They slowed their pace until Ignorance finally caught up. He looked like a guy who thought he had it all figured out—relaxed, confident, maybe even a little smug. He smiled like someone who didn't have a care in the world.

"Hey," Christian said, giving him a nod. "Why so far back?"

Ignorance gave a casual shrug. "I just prefer walking alone—unless the company's really worth it."

Christian shot Hopeful a knowing look but didn't say what he was thinking. Instead, he turned back to Ignorance. "Alright then, since you're here, mind if we talk a bit? How are things between you and God?"

Ignorance beamed. "Great, actually. I'm always thinking about good stuff—God, heaven, all that. It keeps me going."

Christian narrowed his eyes. "Thinking about God and heaven is fine. But that's not enough. Even demons think about those things."

Ignorance frowned, confused. "Yeah, but I *want* those things."

Christian nodded. "Lots of people *want* them. Doesn't mean they'll get there. The Bible even says lazy people want things but never get them."

Ignorance crossed his arms. "Well, I've given up everything for God."

"That's a big claim," Christian said. "How do you know you've really given it all up?"

"My heart tells me so."

Christian raised an eyebrow. "The Bible says, 'He who trusts in his own heart is a fool.'"

Ignorance shook his head. "That verse is about evil hearts. Mine's good."

"And how do you know that?"

"My heart comforts me with hope of heaven."

"Maybe your heart's lying to you," Christian said bluntly. "People can feel good about things they have no real reason to hope for."

Ignorance rolled his eyes. "My heart and my life agree. That's why my hope is solid."

Christian leaned in. "Who told you that?"

"My heart. Again."

Christian sighed. "That's like asking your best friend if you're a thief and just trusting whatever they say. Unless God's Word agrees with your heart, it doesn't count for much."

Ignorance bristled. "Isn't it good to have good thoughts and live by God's commandments?"

Christian nodded. "Yes, but there's a difference between *thinking* you're doing good and actually doing it."

Ignorance folded his arms. "Okay then, what's a good thought about yourself?"

Christian didn't flinch. "One that matches what God's Word says. And it says no one is righteous. None of us naturally want God. Our hearts are messed up—constantly. Unless you recognize that, your 'good thoughts' aren't so good."

Ignorance scoffed. "I'm not buying that my heart is that bad."

"Then you've never had a truly honest thought about yourself," Christian replied. "God's Word also says our paths are messed up—twisted, wrong. If you don't see that, then you're ignoring reality."

Ignorance huffed. "So what do you think about God, then?"

Christian's tone softened. "That He sees us fully. Every hidden thought. Even our best efforts smell like trash to Him. We can't impress Him with good behavior. That's why we need Jesus."

"I believe in Jesus," Ignorance said quickly. "He died for sinners, right? I think God accepts me because I try to obey Him. Jesus helps make my efforts good enough."

Christian stopped in his tracks. "No. That's not saving faith. Real faith doesn't say, 'God accepts me because I try hard.' Real faith says, 'I'm lost without Jesus. Only His perfect life and death can save me—not my effort.' You're trying to mix your obedience with His grace, but that's not how it works."

Ignorance's face twisted in frustration. "So what, we just trust what Jesus did and live however we want?"

Christian shook his head. "You *don't get it*. Real faith changes you. When you understand what Jesus did for you, you don't want to live however. You want to follow Him with everything."

Hopeful spoke up. "Has Jesus ever been revealed to your heart by God?"

Ignorance scoffed. "You're one of *those* guys who talk about 'revelations.' I think all that stuff is just crazy talk."

Christian looked him straight in the eye. "Jesus *has* to be revealed by God. We can't figure Him out on our own. Real faith isn't natural—it's supernatural."

Ignorance stopped walking. "You guys go on. I'm gonna stay here for a bit."

Christian and Hopeful looked at each other, then quietly stepped forward on the path, leaving Ignorance behind.

Teen Commentary

Don't Be "Ignorance"

Let's be real: Ignorance thought he had it all together. He was confident, casual, and totally convinced that he was good with God—because, well, *he felt good about it.* But feelings aren't facts, and that's exactly what Christian was trying to show him.

This scene hits hard because it calls out something so common today: confusing "being spiritual" or "thinking good thoughts" with real faith. Ignorance believed in a *Jesus + me* version of salvation—where Jesus helps, but your good behavior seals the deal. That's not the gospel. The gospel says, "You can't fix yourself, but Jesus can."

Also, notice how Ignorance trusted his heart…a lot. But Scripture tells us the heart can lie. Like, a lot. That's why we need God's Word to measure what's really true.

At the end of the day, it's not about how you *feel* or how many good vibes you send up—it's about knowing who Jesus really is, admitting you're lost without Him, and letting His grace totally wreck and rebuild your life.

Reflection Questions

1. Have you ever assumed you were "good with God" just because you felt okay inside or were trying your best?

2. What's one way you might be trusting your heart more than God's Word?

3. How can you tell the difference between "good intentions" and true saving faith?

4. Do you believe Jesus' righteousness alone is enough to make you right with God? Why or why not?

Scripture Connection

"He who trusts in his own heart is a fool, but he who walks wisely will be delivered."—*Proverbs 28:26 (NKJV)*

Devotional Prayer

Heavenly Father, help me not to lean on my own feelings or thoughts when it comes to knowing You. I don't want to live in ignorance, thinking I'm fine without seeing my real need for Jesus. Open my eyes to the truth of Your Word. Show me where I'm deceived and lead me into real, saving faith that trusts fully in Christ. Make my heart humble, and help me walk in wisdom and truth. In Jesus' Name, Amen.

RIGHT FEAR

The road wound through a sleepy patch of forest, where the trees whispered with the breeze and the sun painted the path in gold and shadow. Christian and Hopeful walked in steady rhythm, their steps light but their conversation heavy with thought.

Behind them, a lone figure limped along—Ignorance, still trailing, still stubborn.

Christian glanced over his shoulder. "Man, it really gets to me," he said, sighing. "That guy… he thinks he's on the right path, but he's headed for a crash."

Hopeful gave a grim nod. "Yeah. Back in our hometown, there were *lots* of people like him—whole neighborhoods full of folks who thought they were 'pilgrims' but were just coasting. If that's how it is where we're from, imagine how it is where *he* started."

Christian shook his head slowly. "The Bible says it straight—'They've been blinded, so they can't even see the truth.'"

They walked in silence for a moment. Then Christian turned to Hopeful. "Hey, real talk—do you think people like him ever feel that inner tug? Like, conviction? That wake-up moment when you realize something's off?"

Hopeful raised an eyebrow. "You're older in the faith. What do *you* think?"

Christian kicked at a rock, then answered. "Yeah, I think they *do*—sometimes. But when it happens, they don't know what to do with it. They feel uncomfortable or scared, and instead of letting that wake them up, they shove it down. They convince themselves they're fine. They silence the alarm."

Hopeful nodded slowly. "Fear can actually be a good thing, huh?"

Christian gave a half-smile. "If it's *right fear*, yeah. That's the kind that pushes you toward God—not away from Him. The Bible says 'The fear of the Lord is the beginning of wisdom.' It's not being afraid of God like He's out to get you, but realizing how holy He is and how *not* holy we are."

Hopeful tilted his head. "So what exactly is right fear, then?"

Christian held up three fingers. "Alright—real simple. One: it starts when you truly get how serious sin is. Two: it drives you straight to Jesus, because you *know* you can't save yourself. And three: it sticks with you. It gives you a deep respect for God and His Word. It keeps your heart soft and your feet steady so you don't drift into stuff that dishonors Him."

Hopeful smiled. "That hits. It's like, not fear that *pushes you away* from God, but fear that *pulls you closer.*"

"Exactly," Christian said. "It makes you *care*. Ignorance doesn't have that. People like him get those gut-check moments from the Holy Spirit, and instead of leaning in, they shove them off. They think it's just the enemy trying to mess with them."

Hopeful looked confused. "Seriously? They think conviction is from the devil?"

"Yep," Christian said. "Or they think it'll ruin their 'faith'—though they don't actually have any. Or they assume they shouldn't feel fear at all, so they fake confidence. Or—and this one's common—they're scared that fear might force them to admit their self-righteousness is trash. So they fight it."

Hopeful's voice dropped. "I remember that. Before I met Jesus for real, I used to brush off those uncomfortable feelings too. I didn't know they were God's mercy trying to wake me up."

They walked a while longer. The air grew cooler, and the path felt lighter somehow.

"Are we almost past this Enchanted Ground?" Hopeful asked.

Christian smiled. "You tired of deep convos?"

Hopeful laughed. "No way! I just wanted to know how much further we've got."

"Just a little bit more," Christian replied. "But hey, let's keep going with this. We've got more to unpack."

Teen Commentary

The Kind of Fear You Shouldn't Ignore

Okay, let's get this straight—*not all fear is bad*. I mean, yeah, there's the kind that keeps you from jumping off rooftops (wise), and there's the kind that keeps you from raising your hand in math class (eh, we've all been there).

But *right fear*? That's something different. It's not about being scared of God like He's out to strike you down with lightning. It's about realizing just how huge, holy, and powerful God is—and how deeply we need Him. It's the kind of fear that says, "Wow, I can't do this on my own. I need Jesus." It's the moment when your heart *wakes up* and stops pretending everything's fine when it isn't.

Here's the deal: God sometimes nudges us with conviction. It's that moment when something you did, said, or thought *just doesn't sit right*. Don't push that away. Don't brush it off or drown it in noise. That conviction? That fear? It might just be God tapping on your heart, saying, "Hey, let's fix this—together."

Ignorance didn't get that. He thought fear meant failure. But right fear? It's the start of something real.

Reflection Questions

1. Have you ever felt convicted or uneasy about something but tried to ignore it? What happened?

2. How can you tell the difference between unhealthy fear and "right fear" that leads you closer to God?

3. Why do you think people resist the feeling of conviction, even when it's meant for their good?

4. What would it look like to respond to God's correction with humility instead of pride?

Scripture Connection

"The fear of the Lord is the beginning of wisdom, and knowledge of the Holy One is understanding."—*Proverbs 9:10 (NIV)*

Devotional Prayer

Heavenly Father, sometimes I'm afraid to face the truth about myself. I try to pretend I'm fine, even when I know something's off. But I don't want to live like that anymore. Teach me to recognize the kind of fear that draws me closer to You. Give me the courage to face conviction and respond with humility. Help me trust Your love, even when You challenge me. Make my heart soft, and keep me close to You. In Jesus' Name, Amen.

Scene 41

BACKSLIDING

They left Ignorance behind, still trailing in the distance, stubborn and self-assured. The forest path grew quiet again, and the hum of cicadas in the trees filled the silence between Christian and Hopeful.

Christian broke it first. "You remember that guy Temporary?"

Hopeful's face darkened. "Yeah. Lived in Graceless, not far from me. About two miles from Honesty, remember? He was roommates with Turnback."

Christian nodded. "That's the one. Dude really seemed fired up at first. Talked about sin, judgment, even cried a few times when we prayed."

Hopeful gave a bitter laugh. "He used to come by my place all the time. Told me he was serious about following God. I really thought he meant it."

"But then," Christian said, "he met Save-Self, and everything changed. He ghosted everyone and slipped right back into his old life."

Hopeful sighed. "It's sad, but it happens. I've been wondering... why do people like Temporary fall away so fast?"

Christian slowed his pace. "Good question. You start. I'll add on."

Hopeful nodded. "Alright. I think first—it's like this: when people get scared of hell or guilt over what they've done, they get really religious *fast*. But it's not because their heart's changed. It's just fear. So, when the fear fades... so does their 'faith.'"

Christian smiled. "Like a sick dog. While it feels awful, it throws up everything it ate. But the moment it feels better? It goes right back to its own vomit."

Hopeful cringed. "Gross, but yeah—accurate."

Christian continued. "What else?"

"Well," said Hopeful, "some people are just too scared of what others will think. Being a real Christian? It's not always cool. So they get hyped when they feel guilty, but once the emotional high fades and they realize faith might actually *cost* them something—they bail."

Christian nodded. "Fear of people can trap you. Big time."

Hopeful ticked off more on his fingers. "There's also pride. They feel embarrassed by how 'uncool' religion looks. They'd rather be admired than be real. And then there's guilt. People like Temporary don't want to face their brokenness every day. It's easier to pretend it's not there."

Christian sighed. "Bottom line? Their heart never changed. It's like a criminal in court. He acts sorry because he's scared of punishment. But give him freedom, and he's back at it. That's not real repentance—it's just fear of consequences."

Hopeful looked thoughtful. "So how do people actually fall away? Like, practically?"

Christian's eyes narrowed as he listed them off.

"First, they stop thinking about God, or death, or eternity.

Then they quit private stuff—prayer, confessing sin, checking themselves.

Next, they avoid passionate Christians—they make them feel uncomfortable.

Then they zone out in church, stop reading Scripture, ditch youth group.

After that, they start criticizing Christians they used to admire—looking for any flaw to justify walking away.

Then, they start hanging out with people who don't care about God at all.

From there, they joke about sin. Gossip. Flirt. Party. Act like nothing matters.

Then they start sinning in public—on purpose.

And finally… they don't even try to hide it anymore."

He stopped, and the woods felt eerily quiet.

Hopeful kicked a stone off the path. "Unless God steps in, that road only leads one place."

Christian looked ahead. "That's why we have to stay alert. Keep walking. Keep praying. And never assume we've 'made it.'"

Teen Commentary

When Faith Fades—And How to Stop It

We've all seen it—or maybe *been* it. Someone gets super into church, cries during worship, posts Bible verses on their story, maybe even tosses their old music or apps. And then… six months later? They're done. Ghosted God. Back to the same crowd, same drama, same junk.

So what happened?

This scene is like Bunyan's "how-to" guide for why people *backslide*—aka, start off strong and then quit their faith walk. Sometimes it starts with fear (hell = scary), but without a real heart change, it fizzles out. Other times, it's about pride, pressure from friends, or just not wanting to feel the weight of conviction anymore.

But here's the truth: real faith isn't built on fear alone. It's built on love. On *relationship*. On a heart that's been flipped upside-down by Jesus.

If you feel yourself slipping—or watching someone else slip—don't ignore it. Backsliding doesn't usually happen all at once. It's a slow drift. One step away. Then another. Until you're way off course and barely remember how you got there.

But the good news? You can always turn back. Right now. God's grace isn't just for the perfect. It's for the prodigals.

Reflection Questions

1. Have you ever felt yourself starting to drift away from God? What were the signs?

2. What "small steps" do you think lead people into big spiritual falls?

3. Who do you surround yourself with—people who help you grow closer to Jesus, or people who pull you away?

4. What's one thing you can do this week to *reignite* your relationship with God?

Scripture Connection

"The dog returns to its vomit, and the sow that is washed returns to her wallowing in the mud."—*2 Peter 2:22 (NIV)*

"The fear of man brings a snare, but whoever trusts in the Lord is kept safe."—*Proverbs 29:25 (NIV)*

Devotional Prayer

Heavenly Father, I don't want to be a Temporary. I don't want to fake it, ride the emotional wave, and then fall away. I want to be rooted in You. Change my heart—not just my habits. Help me spot the signs when I start to drift and give me the courage to turn back. Surround me with people who love You, and help me love You more every day. Keep me close, Jesus. In Jesus' Name, Amen.

Scene 42

THE COUNTRY OF BEULAH

The sun never seemed to set in Beulah.

Christian and Hopeful stepped off the rough path they'd been trudging for days, their shoes caked in dust, shoulders worn from struggle. But now, everything changed. The sky stretched wide and cloudless, its brilliant blue bathing the hills in light. The air was fragrant, like wildflowers after a summer storm. Every breath they took felt like it healed something inside them.

Birdsong filled the air — not just chirping, but melodies that sounded like joy itself. Streams sparkled as they wound through fields of lavender and golden wheat. And the path — straight, clear, glowing faintly — led directly through it all.

Christian let out a laugh. It started soft, like he wasn't sure if it was okay to feel this good, then it spilled out, full and free. "Hopeful," he said, spinning once like a little kid, "this place — it's everything we imagined. And more."

Hopeful nodded, his eyes scanning the horizon. "It feels like we're almost there. The City. I think we can see it."

In the distance, rising above the hills like a dream, was the Celestial City. Its walls shimmered with a glow that made them ache with longing. Gold streets caught the sunlight and threw it back tenfold. The gates looked like they were made from diamonds.

"I... I feel weird," Christian muttered suddenly, gripping his chest. "Like... my heart is too full."

"Same," Hopeful said, his voice soft. "It hurts, but in a good way. Like I'm *homesick*, but I've never even been there before."

They collapsed on a patch of grass beneath a cherry tree, both overwhelmed by the weight of beauty and longing. "If you see my Beloved," Christian whispered through tears, "tell Him I'm love-sick."

Not long after, a man in simple robes — shining subtly like morning dew — approached. He had a gardener's hat slung back on his neck and a pair of pruning shears in one hand.

"These gardens," Christian asked, sitting up, "they're incredible. Who do they belong to?"

"They're the King's," the man said warmly. "Planted for His joy... and for the comfort of weary travelers like yourselves."

He beckoned them in, and they followed. Vines heavy with grapes hung low, and apple trees bent under the weight of fruit. The scent of fresh bread and spices floated from somewhere nearby. "Eat freely," the gardener said. "This part of the journey is for rest."

They wandered through the orchards, sat beneath vine-covered arbors, and finally fell asleep in a patch of lilies. As they slept, they whispered — prayers, dreams, praise — as if the sweetness of this place filled even their dreams with life.

When they woke, the City was closer than ever. The golden reflection of its walls shimmered too brightly to look at directly. The gardener handed them a small glass instrument, like a telescope, through which they could gaze without being blinded.

As they peered through it, two figures approached, their robes glowing like sunlight on water. Their faces were peaceful, bright. Christian and Hopeful stood in awe.

"The King is ready," said one of the men, smiling. "He waits for you at the gate."

Teen Commentary

Welcome to the Edge of Glory

Beulah is basically the last stop before Heaven — and it's awesome. It's that rare moment on your faith journey where everything *clicks*. The struggle? Worth it. The questions? Quieted. The presence of God? Almost *tangible*. You've been through doubts, valleys, and drama, but now you're resting. You can see where you're going. You're surrounded by peace, beauty, and truth.

But here's the thing: Beulah isn't just about Heaven someday — it's a taste of Heaven *now*. It reminds us that God gives us *joy* in the journey, not just at the finish line.

Christian and Hopeful didn't stop because they were lazy — they were finally free to rest because the hardest part was behind them. Maybe you've had "Beulah" moments in your life: a breakthrough at camp, a late-night worship session that made you cry for no reason, or a conversation that just filled your heart.

Beulah is the reminder: *You're almost home. Keep walking.*

Reflection Questions

1. Have you ever experienced a "Beulah moment" — a time when God felt especially close or real?

2. Why do you think God gives us glimpses of Heaven during hard times?

3. How can you build moments of spiritual rest and joy into your daily life?

4. Who do you know that needs to be reminded that rest *is* part of the journey?

Scripture Connection

"No longer will they call you Deserted, or name your land Desolate. But you will be called Hephzibah, and your land Beulah; for the LORD will take delight in you, and your land will be married." — *Isaiah 62:4*

Devotional Prayer

Heavenly Father, thank You for the beauty You let me see along the way. When the path feels endless and hard, remind me of the joy that's coming — and the joy that's already here. Help me to rest in You, to soak in Your love, and to keep walking toward You with hope. Let my heart stay lovesick for Heaven, but faithful here on Earth. In Jesus' Name, Amen.

THE LAST DIFFICULTIES

The sunlight glinted off the water ahead, casting long, golden reflections that danced in ripples. Christian and Hopeful stood side by side, eyes fixed on the wide river that lay between them and the shining City in the distance. The gates of the City sparkled like diamonds, so close—yet now feeling impossibly far.

Two figures in radiant, golden clothing had joined them just before the river. Their faces seemed to glow from within, like they carried the light of the City in their eyes.

"You've come so far," one of them said gently. "You've made it through so many trials. There are only two difficulties left—and then you're home."

Christian blinked at the water. "Is there a bridge somewhere? A boat, maybe?" he asked, scanning the horizon nervously.

The radiant man shook his head. "No bridge. No boat. You have to go through the river. Everyone does—except for a rare few. Enoch. Elijah. The rest must cross by faith."

Hopeful squared his shoulders. "Then let's do it."

But Christian hesitated. The water looked dark. Deep. The idea of sinking... of being overwhelmed...

"What if I can't make it?" Christian whispered. "What if I sink? What if all of this was for nothing?"

Hopeful placed a hand on his shoulder. "We've come this far, haven't we? We didn't fight through the Valley of the Shadow, climb the Hill Difficulty, or survive Doubting Castle to stop now. We're almost there, Christian."

Christian took a breath. Then another. Together, they stepped into the river.

Immediately, Christian stumbled. The cold water surged around him, dragging at his legs. Panic flared in his chest.

"I'm sinking!" he cried. "Hopeful—I can't do this! The waves—they're too strong!"

Hopeful held tightly to his friend's arm. "I can feel the bottom, Christian. It's solid. Hold on to me."

But Christian's eyes were wide with fear. "I don't feel anything but regret. Everything I've done wrong—before I started this journey, even after—I can't stop thinking about it. I think… I think I might not make it after all."

Hopeful tightened his grip. "No, brother. This isn't punishment. This is just fear. Remember what you've seen—how far you've come. God hasn't left you."

Christian was quiet, trembling. He was drowning in more than water.

Hopeful spoke again, firmly but with kindness. "Christian, this is not the end. These waters only test your trust. You *will* get through.

Jesus hasn't left you. Remember what He said: *When you pass through the waters, I will be with you.*"

Christian gasped, as if those words punched through the fog in his mind. "I... I see Him. I see Him! He's here—He's with me!"

With that, something changed. The current seemed to lose its strength. The fear in Christian's eyes began to fade. Step by step, they moved forward together. The bottom felt firm under his feet. His hand clutched Hopeful's arm, but more than that, he held to hope.

They emerged from the river, dripping wet but smiling.

Two shining figures waited on the other side.

"We are here to welcome you," one said, offering a hand. "We serve the King. Come, heirs of salvation."

Christian and Hopeful looked at each other in awe. The weariness of the journey had fallen away. Even their clothes—once travel-worn and dusty—were gone. They felt lighter. Whole.

The path before them led up a hill so high its peak pierced the clouds. But they didn't feel tired. In fact, they almost flew. The two shining guides took them by the arms, and together they climbed, laughing, crying, talking of the wonders to come.

They were homeward bound.

Teen Commentary

Faith in the Deep End

Okay—let's be real. This scene is intense.

Christian is *this close* to reaching the Celestial City (aka Heaven), and boom—there's a river. No bridge. No shortcut. Just faith. And it completely freaks him out.

Ever been there?

Not literally in a river, but in a place where fear takes over? Where everything you've done wrong suddenly plays on repeat in your brain? Maybe you've thought, "Am I even good enough?" or "What if I mess up everything?"

Christian's meltdown in the river is super relatable. He panics. He doubts. But Hopeful—his friend—reminds him of the truth. That God is *still* with him. That fear doesn't mean failure.

And when Christian finally lifts his eyes off the waves and back to God? Peace. Strength. Purpose.

Sometimes the most terrifying moments in life are the ones that reveal just how much we need to hold onto Jesus. The river didn't disappear—but it didn't defeat him either.

Reflection Questions

1. Have you ever had a moment where fear made you forget God's promises? What helped you come back to the truth?
2. What kind of "deep waters" are you walking through right now? Who's your Hopeful—someone reminding you of what's true?
3. Why do you think Christian felt so much doubt right before reaching the City? Have you ever felt that kind of spiritual pressure?
4. What does it mean to walk by faith when you can't see the way clearly?

Scripture Connection

"When you pass through the waters, I will be with you; and when you pass through the rivers, they will not sweep over you." —*Isaiah 43:2 (NIV)*

Devotional Prayer

Heavenly Father, sometimes I feel overwhelmed—like I'm drowning in doubts, fear, or regret. Help me to remember that You never leave me, even when things feel dark. Give me faith to trust You, even when the way forward is scary. Surround me with friends who speak hope and truth, and let me be that kind of friend to others too. Thank You for always walking with me, even through the deepest waters. In Jesus' Name, Amen.

Scene 44

WELCOME

The mountain air shimmered, as if Heaven itself was leaning over to catch a glimpse. Christian and Hopeful stood side by side, breathless—not from exhaustion this time, but from awe. Their journey was over. Behind them lay valleys of despair, battles with temptation, the bitter tears of regret and longing. Before them rose the shining gates of the Celestial City.

Suddenly, the clouds above them swirled with light. A host of brilliant beings—Shining Ones—descended like a symphony of stars. Their robes were brighter than anything earth could hold, and their voices rang out like music made of joy.

One of them stepped forward. "You made it," he said, smiling like the sun. "Because you loved the King and followed Him even when the road was rough, He sent us to walk you home."

From the gate burst forth trumpeters, clad in radiant white, lifting shining horns. They blew a melody that filled the sky—so loud and beautiful it echoed across eternity. Then came the shout from the multitude: "Welcome! Welcome, children of the King! You are called to the Marriage Supper of the Lamb!"

Hopeful's eyes filled with tears. "It's real," he whispered.

Christian nodded, overwhelmed. "It was all worth it."

The Shining Ones surrounded them, guiding them like royal guards. Bells rang from the City beyond the gate. Laughter and singing floated on the wind. They could see others inside—people they'd loved and missed. Faces from long ago, now lit with glory.

The gates stood tall, and above them were golden words that shimmered as they read them: *"Blessed are they that do His commandments, that they may have right to the Tree of Life."*

"Step forward," said a voice from above. Christian and Hopeful held out their scrolls—their certificates of journey, given to them long ago when they first believed. A messenger carried them in.

The King, from within the City, read the scrolls. Then He spoke: "Open the gates. Let the righteous enter in."

As the gates swung wide, light like liquid gold spilled out. Christian and Hopeful stepped forward. In a moment, they were changed—robes of white covered them, and crowns were placed on their heads. Harps were handed to them, not like the ones in cartoons, but instruments that pulsed with living sound.

The entire City erupted in celebration. Every bell rang. Every angel sang. And the King's voice, strong and full of joy, welcomed them: *"Enter into the joy of your Lord."*

Christian looked to Hopeful, and they both lifted their voices in praise:

"Blessing, honor, glory, and power, be to Him who sits on the throne, and to the Lamb forever!"

They walked into streets of gold, surrounded by saints and angels. Joy bubbled up from inside them like a fountain that would never run dry.

At last…they were home.

Teen Commentary

Almost Heaven

Okay, wow. What a moment.

After everything they went through—Christian and Hopeful *made it*. This isn't just some fairy-tale ending. It's a picture of what's real and promised for every believer in Jesus: Heaven. Not clouds and harps in a boring choir, but a vibrant, beautiful place where every tear, every loss, and every hard day gets swallowed up in joy.

This scene shows us what happens when we finally see Jesus face-to-face. Imagine walking through those gates and hearing, *"Well done."* Imagine seeing the people who went before you—the friend who shared their faith, the grandparent who prayed for you. You're not a random person at the door. You're expected. You're *wanted*. You're *home*.

And here's the best part: we don't have to wait until the end of life to start living with Heaven in view. Every step we take toward Jesus today is a step toward that moment. Every decision to trust Him when it's hard is planting seeds that will bloom forever.

Reflection Questions

1. What does "Heaven" mean to you personally—and how does this scene change that perspective?

2. What "scroll" are you writing with your life right now? If you were to meet the King today, what would you want your story to say?

3. How can remembering the hope of Heaven help you when life gets really hard?

4. Who do you hope to see again in Heaven someday—and what would you say to them?

Scripture Connection

"Dear friends, now we are children of God, and what we will be has not yet been made known. But we know that when Christ appears, we shall be like him, for we shall see him as he is." —*1 John 3:2 (NIV):*

Devotional Prayer

Jesus, thank You for the hope of Heaven. Sometimes life is really hard, and it's easy to forget that all of this is leading somewhere amazing. Help me live every day with Your promises in my heart. Keep me faithful when I'm tired, and remind me that I'm never alone on this journey. I want to see You one day—face to face—and hear You say, "Welcome home." Amen.

Scene 45

IGNORANCE COMES TO HIS END

The sun was just starting to rise behind the great gates of the Celestial City, casting golden light across the hills. Birds were singing, trumpets still echoed faintly from the last arrival, and the air buzzed with glory. It was the kind of morning that made you feel like anything was possible.

Then came footsteps—slow, steady, confident.

A teenage guy climbed the final slope toward the gates. His clothes were neat, not worn like those who had journeyed hard. His shoes were spotless. His name was **Ignorance**.

He didn't look tired. In fact, he was smiling, humming to himself as he strolled to the river's edge. There, conveniently waiting, was a boat. A man named **Vain-Hope** leaned lazily on an oar.

"No need to swim," Vain-Hope said with a grin. "I'll get you across. No need to sweat like those other two."

"Nice," Ignorance replied, climbing in. "I knew I didn't need to stress like everyone else. I've always believed in the King, you know. I went to church. Said my prayers. I'm not worried."

The boat glided across the river with barely a ripple. No fear. No struggle. No surrender. No faith. Just smooth, easy drifting.

When Ignorance reached the gates, he looked up at the words carved into gold above them. *"Blessed are they that do His commandments, that they may have the right to the tree of life."* He knocked confidently.

Two guards appeared on the high walls—Shining Ones, radiating light. One of them spoke.

"Where are you from? And why are you here?"

Ignorance straightened. "I've eaten and drank in the King's presence. He taught in our streets. I know who He is. I've always considered myself religious."

The guards nodded slowly. "Show us your certificate—the scroll. The record of your journey."

Ignorance froze. He reached into his coat. Checked all his pockets. Panic flashed in his eyes. "I… uh… hang on…"

"Do you have a certificate?"

No answer.

The Shining Ones looked at each other. One of them bowed his head and turned back toward the City. The other remained still. After a moment, he said softly, "The King will not come down to see you."

Ignorance's jaw dropped. "What? Why not? I *believed*! I was a good person! I *knew* about Him!"

But the Shining Ones didn't argue. Instead, they stepped forward with solemn expressions, and gently but firmly took hold of him.

"What's happening?" Ignorance cried, struggling now. "This has to be a mistake!"

The next thing he knew, they were lifting him. Not into the City, but away from it—high into the sky. The golden gates grew smaller beneath him as they flew toward a dark, jagged hill off to the side. A narrow, twisted door opened in the mountain.

No celebration. No music. No welcome.

Just silence.

They placed him at the threshold. The door closed behind him.

And in that moment, I realized: There's a path to hell that runs right past the gates of Heaven.

Then I woke up.

Teen Commentary

Too Close to Miss It

Oof. This one hits hard.

Ignorance wasn't some wild rebel. He wasn't out partying or mocking God. He was *religious*. He said the right things, did some good stuff, even knew who Jesus was. But here's the problem—he *never really followed* Jesus. He believed *about* the King, but he never surrendered his life to Him. He took the easy road and assumed that was enough.

It's like showing up to a concert with a fake ticket. You can know the songs, wear the merch, even follow the band on social media—but if your ticket's not real, you're not getting in.

This scene isn't meant to scare you—it's meant to *wake you up*. You don't have to be perfect, but you *do* need a real relationship with Jesus. Not just Sunday habits or good vibes. Not secondhand faith. **You need to know Him—and let Him know you.**

Reflection Questions

1. Do you ever find yourself just "going through the motions" when it comes to faith? Why is that dangerous?

2. What's the difference between knowing *about* Jesus and truly following Him?

3. If you stood at the gates today, would you be confident in your relationship with Jesus—or just hoping it's enough?

4. Who in your life might be like Ignorance—close to the truth, but not surrendered to it?

Scripture Connection

"Not everyone who says to me, 'Lord, Lord,' will enter the kingdom of heaven, but only the one who does the will of my Father who is in heaven… Then I will tell them plainly, 'I never knew you. Away from me, you evildoers!'" —*Matthew 7:21-23 (NIV)*

Devotional Prayer

Heavenly Father, I don't want to fake it. I don't want to just look religious on the outside—I want to know You for real. Show me where I've been pretending, coasting, or trusting in my own goodness instead of Your grace. Help me follow You with everything I am, even when it's hard. I want to be Yours, all the way to the end. In Jesus' Name, Amen.

Conclusion

THE FINAL WORD

The fire had died down to glowing embers. The sky outside the window was shifting to that deep, dreamy blue that happens just before dawn. The storyteller leaned back in his chair, stretching a little, and looked around the room at the teens who had been listening to him for what felt like hours—but no one had moved.

Some were leaning forward, elbows on knees. Others sat back, brows furrowed, deep in thought. A few had tears in their eyes. The story of the Pilgrim—the journey, the battles, the friendships, the traps, and the final gates—had hit different.

The storyteller glanced down at his worn notebook, the pages covered in scribbles and sketches, and then looked up.

"That's the dream," he said softly, closing the book. "Now it's your turn."

He paused, letting the silence speak for a moment.

"Don't just laugh at the strange names or get hung up on the old-school language. Don't think it's just a made-up tale. If all you see are weird metaphors and cool-sounding places, you've missed the point."

He stood and stepped toward the center of the room.

"Dig deeper. Look past the surface. Christian's journey? It's *your* journey. His struggles with doubt, peer pressure, distractions, guilt—that's all real. Every trap he faced, every choice he made—it's stuff we all deal with. The enemy still whispers lies, and the King still calls people home. This wasn't just a story. It was a mirror."

The storyteller's voice dropped lower, his eyes serious now.

"If something in the story seemed off, feel free to toss it out. But don't throw away the gold just because it came wrapped in an old package. Truth doesn't expire just because the slang is outdated."

He looked around the circle one last time.

"So… what will you do with it? Will you just say, 'Cool story, bro,' and scroll on? Or will you take a real look at your own journey and start walking toward the King?"

He turned and walked out the door, leaving only silence—and the weight of the question behind.

Teen Commentary

Unpacking the Dream

This scene is like Bunyan stepping out of the book and handing *you* the mic. He's saying, "Okay, you heard the story. Now what are you gonna do with it?"

It's super easy to treat stuff like this as just another Christian allegory—old-school, kind of weird, full of metaphors you half get and half roll your eyes at. But Bunyan *knew* people would feel that way. That's why this ending is so real. He's saying: "Don't let the old-timey packaging keep you from finding truth."

Think of it like this: ever watched a TikTok that started off weird, but by the end had you in your feels? That's this story. It's not about the talking characters or fantasy cities—it's about the decisions you're making *right now*. Where are you heading? Who are you trusting? Are you just playing religious games—or actually following Jesus?

Reflection Questions

1. What part of *The Pilgrim's Progress* felt the most real to you? Why?

2. Have you ever dismissed something important because it seemed "old" or "not cool"?

3. What's one metaphor or moment from the story that you think applies to your life right now?

4. What does "preserving the gold" from the story look like in your faith journey?

Scripture Connection

"For the word of God is alive and powerful. It is sharper than the sharpest two-edged sword… It exposes our innermost thoughts and desires." —*Hebrews 4:12 (NLT)*

Devotional Prayer

Heavenly Father, thank You for stories that challenge and stretch me. Help me not to ignore truth just because it looks different or feels uncomfortable. Open my eyes to what You're saying through it all. Show me where I am on the journey—and how to walk closer with You every day. Let me not miss the gold. In Jesus' Name, Amen.

Epilogue

YOUR JOURNEY BEGINS

Christian's story may have ended, but yours is just beginning.

Like Christian, you will walk through valleys of doubt, wrestle with fears, battle despair, and face temptations dressed up as comfort, success, or popularity. You will meet people who help you and others who try to pull you off the narrow path. But through it all, remember: **you are not walking alone**.

Jesus is not just waiting for you at the Celestial City. He walks beside you now. He guides you, strengthens you, and reminds you of who you are and where you're going.

This book isn't just a cool old story rewritten for a new generation—it's a mirror for your life. Every obstacle Christian faced is something you'll face too, in your own way. Every truth he discovered is yours to claim. Every step he took toward God is an invitation for you to take one too.

So ask yourself:

- What burdens am I carrying?
- What distractions are pulling me away from truth?
- Who am I becoming on this journey?

There's still time to lay your burden down at the cross. Still time to walk forward in faith. Still time to say "yes" to the King who never stops loving you.

May this book have done more than entertain you. May it stir something deep in your soul—a longing for truth, a hunger for purpose, a boldness to walk the narrow road. You have a calling. You have a destination. You have a Savior.

Now…
Go live your journey!

A Prayer for Salvation

Jesus, I believe You are the Son of God. I believe You died for my sins and rose again so I could be forgiven and made new. I confess that I've gone my own way, and I ask for Your mercy. Please forgive me, save me, and lead me from this day forward. I want to follow You on this journey. I give You my life. Amen.

Ready for the road? You're not alone. The King walks with you.

Next Steps on Your Journey

1. **Tell someone.** If you prayed the salvation prayer, don't keep it to yourself. Share it with a parent, mentor, youth leader, or trusted Christian friend.

2. **Get a Bible and read it.** Start with the Book of John. It's a great way to get to know Jesus personally.

3. **Find a church or youth group.** Following Jesus is a team journey. You were never meant to do it alone.

4. **Pray daily.** Just talk to God. Share your heart, your questions, your highs and lows. He listens.

5. **Keep growing.** Explore devotionals, Bible studies, and resources that help you understand your faith more deeply. This story may have ended—but your adventure is just beginning. Check out this highly recommended *3-Year Bible Chronological Daily Devotional* (Scan QR Code below)